THE TEENAGE WORRIER'S
PANICK DIARY

Want to know what other Teenage Worriers think about the books? Here are some snippets from letters sent to Letty...

'We are writing to congratulate you on writing such a fantastic book. We think it is a truthful straightforward guide to teenage life. You cover absolutely everything that any teenager – worrier or not – needs to know' *Caroline and Sarah, Edinburgh*

'It's as if you're talking to a friend... All of your Worriers books are cool and super great, fantastico!' *Kirby, North Yorkshire*

'You seem to have made a step towards cutting down on split ends, fashion victims, nailbiting, trips to the doctors and all manner of other worries for teenagers who still, after millions of years of evolution, can't find anyone who understands, gives advice and can crack you up too' *Laura, Lancashire*

'Your book has taught me a lot and I am pleased to know that I am in fact normal... Say hi to Rover for me, she is sooooooooo sweet' *Rena, Norfolk*

'Really kool and cheered *moi* up <u>no end</u> to know I'm not alone' *Maddi, Norfolk*

'So true to life and the illustrations are hilarious' *Emily, Kent*

'I find your books very funny and helpful. I used to worry all the time, but since I discovered Letty Chubb, I don't!' *Jack, East London*

THE TEENAGE WORRIER'S

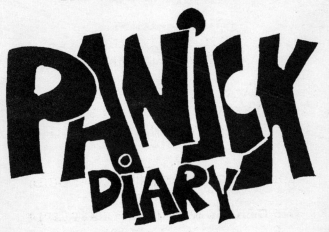

PANICK DIARY

Ros Asquith

as Letty Chubb

CORGI BOOKS

THE TEENAGE WORRIER'S PANICK DIARY
A CORGI BOOK : 0 552 147761

First publication in Great Britain

PRINTING HISTORY
Corgi edition published 2000

1 3 5 7 9 10 8 6 4 2

Set in 11½pt Linotype Garamond

Corgi Books are published by Transworld Publishers,
61–63 Uxbridge Road, London W5 5SA,
a division of The Random House Group Ltd,
in Australia by Random House Australia (Pty) Ltd,
20 Alfred Street, Milsons Point, Sydney, NSW 2061, Australia,
in New Zealand by Random House New Zealand Ltd,
18 Poland Road, Glenfield, Auckland 10, New Zealand
and in South Africa by Random House (Pty) Ltd,
Endulini, 5a Jubilee Road, Parktown 2193, South Africa

Made and printed in Great Britain by
Cox & Wyman, Reading, Berkshire

Unmade Bed,
Sleepy Hollow,
Transylvania,
Brobdignag,
Bazoom-free-zone,
Surrounded-by-newsagents-packed-with-mountainous
  bazooms,
Valley of the Shadow of Banana,
ACNE-ON-THAMES.

Dearest Reader(s),

Mr Patel has stopped selling fudge. He still sells Busty
Babes *and* Wet Shellsuits, *but he says there is no call for
fudge. Now I will have to spend 40p on a bus, just to get fudge.
Would campaign about this, if I had the energy, but as you see
from above address, am still lingering in sub-zero yuniverse
twixt horror and glume lit, from time to time, by spindly
flicker of Hope.*

What is the horror, you ask?

*A list too long, dear friends, to be listed without an army of
secretaries. If I touched the tip of the icedberg it would include:
spotz, allergies, cold sores, failure of all my plans to be werld-
shattering film-maker, and, oh, how can I mention it?
LUMING GCSEs. On top of all that, there is a war on and I'm
Worried the Current Situation will get werse . . .*

*All right, I'm more Worried about the war than the fudge,
but it's not kule to say so.*

What is the glume?

*Luming acne. Lack of luming bazooms. Even werse, loss
of belurved Adam Stone, for ever.*

What is the Hope?

As those few of you who read ye grate Greek Myths in primary skule may recall, there was once a naughty gurl called Pandora who opened a forbidden box. Out of this box flew all the pestilences of the world: Famine, War, Plague, banana itself (sorry, but I still can't write that werd about dying that rhymes with 'breath', so you'll just have to get used to me writing 'banana' instead) and, I expect, cold sores, divorcing parents and banged funny bones, also.

BUT, before the lid of the box was closed, just one more thing fluttered out to chase the others. And this fragile but beautiful thing was HOPE. HOPE made all the other things possible to bear. It is hard to imagine where the yuman race wld be without HOPE, and impossible to imagine where I wld be.

But you'll learn about my hopes in no time if you progress with this, my NEW three-month DIARY, in which I intend to conquer fear, Worry, and Panick for good and step brightly into Spring.

Nachurally, I am including my New Year's Resolutions (just slightly updated from my last diary) in order to aid me with my grate task. Will I get back on the Fantastic film course and make my fortune? Will the handsomest boy in the werld (who I have aksherlly MET) prove to be the One For Me? Will I finally learn how to boil an egg?

Read on . . .

Lurve,

Letty Chubb x

UPDATE ON . . . MOI

Me
15-year-old telegraph pole (spotted)

Family
Two unmarried adults who claim to
be my parents (aksherlly, of course, I
am Astra, star child of a lion
and a witch). PLUS two brothers:
Benjy, a small round one who is scared
of FLOORS (yes), and
Ashley, who has gone off
to Oxford to rule werld.

Grannies
Granny Chubb: poor
and cuddly, with
soul of Nelson
Mandela.
Granny Gosling: posh and brittle
with soul of Attila the Hen.

I l♥ve
Granny
Chubb true
L.C. ♥ G.C.

Pets

Rover: Lurve of my LIFE.
Kitty: bane of my life.
Horace: Benjy's gerbil, bore of my life.

Rover

Best Frendz

Hazel: Blonde bombshell in lurve with a gurl.
Aggy: black brainiac in lurve with Einstein.
Spiggy: loose-limbed Ozzie in lurve with LIFE (puke)

Spiggy Aggy Hazel

Skule

Sluggs Comprehensive: Lives down to its name.

BOYZ
Read on . . .

New Improved Resolutions

1) Write in this diary every day
No prob. Who but this diary truly understands the mysteries of my soul? Who else have I got to talk to? Yah boo self pity Etck.

2) Clean teeth twice a day
Since I can never get into bathrume, which is filled with cursing adults or small brother Benjy, Worried that the loo is a door to another even more scary werld than this. I have decided to take glass of water, toothbrush and paste into own rume. Will keep you updated on success or otherwise of this plan. Bet you can't wait.

3) Limit spot, zit and pluke examinations to once every two days
Am V. Pleased, as have reduced rate from six times daily to five times daily. Partly due to bathroom situation outlined above and lack of other mirrors in our hovel.

4) Limit bazoom measuring to once a week
Current rate, four times daily. They are in fact 2 cm smaller today than yesterday. Tried Wonderbra but cld only Wonder what to put in it.

5) Only measure nose every month instead of weekly
Have decided, only solution is to never stand sideways. Luckily, film directors often have big hooters, so once I have joined their ranks I will feel able to show profile.

12

6) Stop reading krap magazin
Teendreems Etck
YES! Have bought New Year
possibly just plain mental) gesture
generations the junk we Teenage
consume.

7) Read V. Good bukes to improve Mind, starting with
War and Peace **and** *Catch 22*
Think End of War is L. Chubb's task. Why didn't werld
leaders just do that for New Year's Resolution? Wld have
been perfectly easy to Just Say NO.

**8) Do homewerk on day it's set instead of whole week's
werth on Sun at 11 pm**
Er.

9) Improove speling
Vitel tarsk. Unforchunatly,
spel chek on this pre-war
komputer not werking yet.

Katt
~~Kat~~
~~CKatt~~
~~CKat~~
cat ✓

10) Keep rume tidy
Hahaha.

11) Be nice to Benjy
Hohoho.

NB. V. gude spelling
exercise is to see
how many WRONG
spellings you can make

**12) Save every speck of money for Granny Chubb's
Spectacles Endeavour (aiming to buy her a pair for
Easter)**
On Christmas Day, G. Chubb told the lamp stand how
much it had grown, so this task even more urgent.

...top being superstitious
Have left out the number between 12 & 14, which is not a V. Good sign . . .

15) As above, cure one nervous habit each month, starting with having to touch the floor twice whenever I drop something
Well, at least it's not as bad as Benjy, whose floor phobia means he tries not to touch the floor, ever. We will have to fill our hovel with rope ladders and trapezes soon, like the monkey cage at the zoo.

16) Be nice about my Only Mother's paintings
Very nicely suggested she shld try painting something real, like other old ladies do: flowers, or apples. She is sulking.

17) Ditto about my Adored Father's writing
Told Dad he might do better with a bonk-buster rather than another long sad story of his poverty-stricken yoof Etck. I think he took the point as he immediately rushed out to buy lotz of issues of *Busty Babes*.

18) Be More Caring and Sharing with My Frendz
As long as they are more caring and sharing with me.

19) Keep Up with Werld Events
And I don't mean wot Posh and Beckham did on New Year's Eve . . .

20) Add one new werd to vocabulary each day as part of on-going Self-Improvement course
That's enuf resolutions – Ed.

Sat Jan 2

'What a pity it is that people have to kill sausages,' sighed Benjy, gazing at his breakfast plate.

He'll be a veggie soon and the fridge'll be stuffed with tofu curd and extra-live yoghurt that jumps out and bites your hand off, like the Creature from the Swamp. Cld be a welcome change from the usual contents of eighteen cans of Old Bastard lager and a single Budgie Nugget.

But what about plant life? Feel fragile at thort of slaughtering plants to make breakfast cereal. Poor little ears of wheat, waving about, doing nobody any harm, until the Grimme Reaper appears and shreds their little lives. Poor little flaked corns. Poor little crisped ricies. Tragick tiny baby carrots, murdered in their beds to stuff the organic fude counter . . .

And another thing. Poor little muffins, wrenched from tragick ears of corn, cruelly ground in dark Satanic mills . . .

'Letty. Stop buttering your brother.'

It's strange how the mind plays tricks. Benjy often looks so much like a muffin, it's amazing I didn't butter and eat him years ago. It would have been kinder to the environment, too.

'If you want muffins, the shop's just five minutes down the road.'

'Other people's mothers buy them muffins.' I wipe unbidden tear from distant end of voluminous hooter.

'Letty, whassa matter?' slurs Benjy.

'Whassa matter? Whassa matter? What do you care? Nobody cares.' I slam out of rume.

I can hear my mother saying, 'Ooh. Someone got out of bed the wrong side. She IS in a state.'

'Period,' says Benjy firmly.

I think Personal and Social edukashon can start too young. Now even five-year-olds think perfectly normal mude swings are due to periods.

In the depths of my pokey rume, I confess that I have Reasons to be In A State.

As Follows:

1) Will brilliant arty director Alfonsa Rossellini let me go back on brilliant Arty Film Course?

Alfonsa Rossellini is the 'glamorous and brilliant' (as reviewed by sweaty lecherous film Critique Johnathan Woss) director who spotted a one-candlepower glimmer of talent in *moi* and who therefore lit the fuse to dreams of my meteoric career in Hollywood . . . I mean my career as V. Serious and Werthy documentary director revealing Vicious Underbelly of Contemporary Society Etck. She is in charge of the New Directions (Yeah, Yeah, I've done that nude erections joke already and It is V. Embarrassing) Film Skule course. If I get back on the course I might be able to gettalife even without 2 & 3 below.

2) Have done zilch werk for mock GCSEs.

My skule is stupid enuf to do these one term before the real ones so you have no time to get any better. If only they had done them last term, then I wld know how badly I am going to do and could have just jumped off cliff already and saved everyone time and trouble Etck.

3) Will I see Mystery Boy again?

You will want the details . . . or if not, here they are anyway . . .

Here is all I know: Mystery Boy is about five feet 10 inches tall, with eyes a mix of sea green and ocean blue, very dark but with flecks of gold in, er, a bit like the ocean ruffled by a breeze with floating specks of sand catching the glinting sunlight . . . his hair . . . soft, thick, the colour of, wait for it . . . vanilla fudge . . .

His name (don't larf, he can't help it) is Basil. Basil Barrington.

So. I was standing with Hazel at the New Year party when Aggy introduced us and he blew me a kiss. Is this enuf on which to build my dreams? But . . . I felt our eyes were burning into each other's souls.

Decide, only one way to find out if he Cares. If feathers in pillow come out right, it will all be OK.

'He loves me, He loves me not.'
He Loves Me! Yessss!

Was attempting to hoover up results of lurve-feather experiment when bag erupted. Was taking binbag of feathers out to bin as slinky new milkman came whistling up path.

'I see tarring and feathering's back,' he japed.

'Chickens. Who'd have 'em?' I japed cheerily back. Kwick glance in mirror revealed astonishingly large number of feathers attached to mug. How did they get there? Oh well, can cross milkman off potential boyfrend list. Whistle off to shop for hoover bag. Will get eggs, hoover bags, muffins. Will return Benjy's water-bomb arsenal. (*NB* **New werd: Arsenal.** Is not only futeball team and London tube station. It also means a store of weapons. Benjy thinks it sounds like 'bum'n'everything', which is why he supports Spurs). Will make buttered muffins for tea. Will get honey, too.

He loves me! Yesss!

What a byootiful werld. Tra la.

9 pm. Unbeleeevable.

Basil Barrington, his very self, came round during the five minutes that I was at the shop. My mother quite gurlish as she described his smart suit and 'well spoken, polite manner'. Normally praise from Only

19

Mother of this sort wld send yrs truly screaming to hang out with oiks, crack addicts Etck. But I can't help feeling warm glow of hope that I will be allowed out with old Mystery Boy whenever I want. Also, imagine Only Mother noted his fudge-coloured wig, manly twinkle, elegant limbs Etck and was influenced by last rush of hormones before she succumbs to twinsets and a blue rinse.

Sun Jan 3
COOKING, GRANNY CHUBB

Slept V. Well on non-allergic pillow. Will not use feathers again. Only sneezed about six times this morning but that's prob because I woke up with Rover on my face.

Off to Granny Chubb's for cooking lesson. She teaches me how to open sardine can. These are OK unheated (the sardines, not the can) but if you are heating them, heat them right through she sez 'Cos a half warmed fish is as useless as a half formed wish' arf arf. Smell makes me feel sick, but Rover V. Interested, makes noise like car with broken exhaust. Not sure I'll take Rover next time, as she eats half the stuff we make which leaves G. Chubb short of nosh.

Ring Aggs to tell her about Basil.

'Aggs. I'm in Love. Tell me it's OK.'

'It's OK.'

'Thanks. Is that all?'

'Look, Letty, he must be OK if he shares a flat with Junior. Junior is the nicest bloke in the world. Junior used to push me on swings when I was three, used to be ever so kind to my mum . . .' Here Aggs broke off to have a little cry.

'Yeah. But Basil? Has he got a gurlfrend?'

'Known him since I was three. He was in playgroup with Quincey.'

'Yes, well we were all in playgroup once Aggs. What else?'

'Dunno. Got a flash job. Internet. Makes loads of virtual money. Got a virtual car and everything. Quite handsome I suppose, if you like that sort of thing.'

Ah. I get it. She's jealous.

'But Aggs. Listen. Has he got a gurlfriend?'

'Dunno. OK. I'll ask Junior.'

'Aggs, you're the best.'

'I know.'

Hazel comes round to cry.

She is missing Mandy.

I can see that Mandy moving all the way to Scotland is going to be a Problem that won't go away. I must be careful not to let my Dreamz of Mystery Boy and rehearsing Oscars acceptance speech in front

21

of mirror push thoughts of poor Abandoned Hazel from my mind. Being so Byootiful, she makes Extra Speshully good Tragick Heroine, but I feel suggestions that she might star in my major Epick film re Lesbian Lurve Denied by Cruelle Werld wld not go down well at the moment . . .

Go to bed, brane churning with Hopes and Dreamz Etck.

2 am. Outrageous banging and crashing. Stumble downstairs. Only Mother had got there first and was wrestling with the front door, which has been the only thing to do with it since DIY-Dad fixed the locks. DIY-Dad fell into the hall, as wild eyed as the phantom horseman, with oozing mud clinging to him and twigs in his wig.

'What the hell have you been doing?' screamed Mother. 'Thank GOD you're alive!' and she burst into tears.

'Doing? What do you think I've been doing? I've been dining with my agent.'

'But look at yourself! Did you fall in something?'

'Alice, you are so advertent, that's what I love about you.' (**NB new werd newsflash: Advertent.** Means observant, I gather. Writers can be so sarcastick.)

'But you're only wearing a vest! You'll catch a dreadful cold!'

'Cold?! What is cold? Innocent civilians are dying

Out in that Wicked real World out there; millions starve and she worries about a sneeze. Why must I live with such a small-minded woman? She'll be talking about pelmets next.'

Pelmets? But we knew better than to ask more, especially as Benjy had now appeared at the top of the stairs and was complaining his carpet had turned into an omelette.

As far as I could see, Father had fallen in a vat of whisky. He took a huge swig from a flask of the same that he Worryingly had in his trouser pocket, and stumbled upstairs, followed by fretting mother.

Mother surged glumily back downstairs with an armful of sodden clothes which she hung in front of the one-bar electric fire. Central heating, as usual, on blink. I made her a cup of cocoa and retired miserably with Benjy into fitful sleep.

But not for long.

Was woken by gharstly shouting:

'Not more whisky. You'll kill yourself!'

'Itsh Lucozade. Anyway, I'm insured.'
Etck.

Tried putting bedclothes over hed, but after a while became fearful for lives of loved ones and ventured into their rume. It was a horrible sight. My father, coughing, sneezing, and swigging whisky, was ranting away like King Lear.

'Cold, cold,' he was shouting. 'Is there no bloody heating in this house? Thought it was not the moment to remind him he'd been 'fixing' it for three weeks.

'Dad!' I shouted.

'Who are you?' he asked, and fell asleep.

'My God,' muttered Mother. 'I haven't seen him that bad all year. Don't Worry, Letty, he'll feel better in the morning.'

Was about to point out it was only three daze into the year when Benjy came hurtling into the rume, screaming: 'FIRE FIRE FIRE. Daddy on fire!'

'No dear, Daddy in bed,' soothed Mother.

But there was a distinctly foggy atmosphere.

'Oh my GOD! The clothes!' screamed Mother, hurling herself across the prone body of my once Adored Father and clasping her baby chick (Benjy, not *moi*, who is gangly ugly duckling too old for hugs) to her breast.

'Wake up, Dad!' I shook him violently.

'Whosser matter?' he mumbled, stirring.

'The house is burning down.'

'Warm now,' he said and fell asleep.

Mother by this time had calmed down, rung the fire brigade, removed the smouldering clothes, turned off all the electricity.

Eight blokes in yellow oilskins and helmets arrived ten minutes later. The Fire Brigade is a wonderful thing. Firemen are wonderful.

'Not a good idea tryin' to dry off clothes soaked in surgical spirit, mate,' was all one cheerfully said.

All the neighbours poured out into the street. Even Mrs Scrooge offered us half a biscuit.

Neighbours are wonderful.

It's a wonderful world.

We are alive. We could have been burned to a crisp. Basil and I wld never have made Byootiful Musick together. He wld just have read of *moi* as a footnote in the paper after they had found only smouldering foot of El Chubb.

Ugh! Sometimes when you let yuk thoughts into ye brane you can't get them out again.

Mon Jan 4

Bank Holiday, Scotland
BACK TO SKULE. MOCK GCSEs
BEGIN TOMORROW, GLUME, DUME ETCK
BASIL COUNTDOWN: 26 DAYS

'Is there any chance at all of a little muesli and sympathy?' asked Father.

'None,' said Mother, slamming cupboards.

'I have a headache and think I have tuberculosis coming on.'

'You have a hangover and are not fit to father children.'

'If you can't tell the difference between a hangover and a dangerous disease, you are not fit to mother children.'

I sloped off glumly, wondering what it must be

like to be in a functional family where children chirrup their way merrily to skule with shiny faces and tummies full of orange juice and organick muffins.

Two New boys in form 11F. Jack Spriggs is very chirpy, with freckles. He sat next to Spiggy all day making jokes. First time I've seen her smile since being dumped by rat fink Daniel. The other boy, Josef, is V. Quiet, solemn kid. Refugee from war zone. Old Portillo sez we've got to be nice to refugees but he's always complaining about how they wreck Sluggs's league table results. I offered Josef a piece of fudge and he jumped out of his skin.

When I get home, there is a message from one of the two persons in whose hands the shape of El Chubb's future is but putty.

No, not Mystery Boy. But almost as exotick. Alfonsa Rosselini has written to say she is letting me go on film course again. Sez: I have obvious talent.

Amazing.

'I understand your toil and strife, Letty, and that you are serious about this very great and wonderful art form: the magic of cinema is within your grasp. Do not fail me this time . . .'

She would bring that up. It was just a little misunderstanding about my first venture into the werld of the big screen. How was I to know the subjects of my heartrending examination of life on the underside were fakes?

26

But she likes me.

And she is V. Clever. And she's letting me back on the course, tee heee teee ha! Now I will have to think V. Hard. The course starts on Jan 15, which leaves loads of time to prepare Etck. Maybe cld use some of my V. Hard werk as part of GCSE? Or maybe, dream of dreams, I can make really good, deep, meaningful, cutting edge, Save-the-Poor film and can win the £2,000 best film prize and leave skule for ever? YES.

Happiness is around the corner.

Or, possibly even nearer than that.

How can it be that Unhappiness and Glume can spread its slimey glupe all over you for months on end without Respite and then the Werld can turn to blazing sunshine and dazzling colours all at once?

Because . . . first Alfonsa's letter and then . . . Basil rings.

I wldn't say it was quite as long and lazily-Lerving a conversation as I might have wished. But what he did say was nothing short of Totally Mindblowing.

'Letty, I know you love Adam,' I heard those dark chocolate tones come purring down the line, 'but when I saw you at the party I thought, Adam is a fool. How can he pass up on such a gorgeous creature? . . .'

(*What?* Gorgeous? *Moi?* Am I hearing right? Does he need an eye test?)

'Splfft.'

'You OK?'

'Mssplgt.'

'Shall I ring back? I think there's something wrong with the line.'

'NO! Spglt! YES! Ring back any time! Can I see you now?' (Was that me saying that?)

'Look I want to see you now, this moment, yesterday if I could, but I have to go away on urgent business for a month – something a bit hush-hush in fact, but please, please say you'll meet me the minute I get back.'

'Oh, yes. Sure.' (Is this cool or what? I don't even say Adam dumped me). *Going away on business for a month. Something a bit hush-hush* . . . hmmm. Man of Mystery or what? Business! I don't think I've ever talked to anybody who's in a business, except Only Father's agent who's always complaining that if Dad doesn't pull his finger out he'll be out of business.

And Basil is in the business of the future. The Internet, Cyberspace, Virtual Stinking Richness! He is bringing the Global Village together, showing The Werld how to be a better place!

He'll be back on Sat Jan 30th. At 3.30. Gadzooks. I have a boyfrend who is the best-luking boy in the yuniverse and also rich. Is this a dream? Pinch self hard and find, owing to large resulting contusion, that it is not. Good. A month is good. Will give *moi* time to climb into new skin, face Etck for first date. Also to check out he is not two-timing wife and kids Etck (you can tell I am an old cynical woman-of-the-werld by now) and to concentrate on gharstly mock GCSEs (mockery, mockery).

Tue Jan 5

Interesting Fact: Amy Johnson, grate woooman aeronaut, was drowned in the Thames on Jan 5 1941. Wot a way to go. So much for Fear of Flying, then.

The Current Situation is getting worse and all the boyz are obsessed with latest battle stuff, talking about UN, guerrillas, laser-guided missiles, smart bombs, minimal collateral damage Etck Etck.

Josef is not joining in. He is sitting V. Quietly in the corner, drawing. Decide, in 'be nice to refugees' mode, to try to talk to him. He lets me look at his drawing. It is of a man in fatigues, armed to the teeth, cartridge belts all over him Etck, but smiling and extending a hand.

'Who's that?' I ask.

'It's our local barber,' says Josef.

'What does he do, shoot your hairs off one by one?'

Josef gave me a blank look. 'He used to give me a sweet just like that, after a haircut.'

'Then why do you draw him like this?'

'It's how he was dressed when he came to shoot my father.'

...

29

I found myself thinking of the gap between the Boyz I knew and this Boy from another werld so hard that it was impossible to think about anything else all day. Were they from different werlds? Or the same one..?

I realized this had to be the subject of my film...

This is a V. Fashionable idea akshually, as all the mad blokes who think feminism's caused all their problems, are writing about How it Feels to Be a Boy, whether it is essential to get your share of bone-crunching violence, manic shouting, power of Life or Banana over others Etck in order to feel Truely Alive as fully functioning Male Etck. Maybe it is because Gurlz have had the power to create New Life within them, and the closest Boyz can get is at least to be able to say they could take it away again if they felt like it.

So, talking to boyz about war is a V. V. Gude idea. Yeah. Will interview boyz about how they feel. Then I will intercut their moving and heartrending fears or macho tough talk with even more moving and tragic pix of war-wounded, weeping mothers Etck.

But what will I do about Josef? How can I possibly interview him?

Put inconvenient guilty thorts out of mind. Remember practical advantages of this momentous Decision:

1) Will give me a chance to interview most handsome boyz at Sluggs.
I mean, ahem, oldest boyz.
2) Can also go to the posh boyz skule.
Sure old Daniel will let me talk to a couple of his mates. Kule. But I will need a video camera this time. Unless I just use a tape and still photos of the boyz? Mmmnhh. Tough.

Sat up V. Late writing ideas for film. Can do GCSE revision in my next life.

Wed Jan 6
Epiphany.
Babysit.
Vile exams all day.
Basil Countdown: 24 Days

UN soldiers have just bombed a hospital by mistake.

Mother has got her New Year calendar up. It will stay on Jan 6th until April. 'Calendars were originally invented,' sez my Father, 'to remember to celebrate religious festivals.'

Oh, I see. Perhaps God got fed up waiting around in empty churches for Ye Faithful to turn up, only to find out they were all down the pub, and so sent a message to the Chosen Ones attached to a bolt of lightning saying 'go down Smith's and get a calendar Ye Forgetful Twits or I will rain down famine, pestilence, unsolvable computer games Etck.'

'And today,' concludes Father, as we doze over our poor murdered flaked corns, 'is Twelfth Night.'

Oh Pluke. That means we have to get the decorations down or it's seven years of bad luck. Or is that mirrors? Enyway, take a few cards down before skule, to show willing and remind mother to do the rest.

In maths I told Jack Spriggs the story about my dad leaving the 'h' out of Ms Farthing's name in a sick note and how she's been vile to me ever since. It is werse, because she does fart rather a lot.

'Yes indeedy,' says Jack. 'You know what mummy bales of cotton say to their baby bales of cotton?'

'Eh?'

'They say: if you're a good little bale of cotton, you'll grow up to be a lovely fresh crisp checked curtain blowing in a summery breeze. But if you're a BAD little bale of cotton, you'll grow up to be the gusset of Ms Farthing's knickers.'

I snort. He snorts. Spiggy and Aggy snort.

'Enjoying a joke, Scarlett? Would you like to share it with us?' asks Ms Farthing.

'No, miss. Thank you.'

Now I've got to feel sorry for poor little bales of cotton, too.

Thur Jan 7

VILE EXAMS ALL DAY
BASIL COUNTDOWN: 23 DAYS

Was in the library today during brief respite from
Vile exams, scribbling the initials 'BB' all over my
history essay, when Brian lurched up, smirking.
Covered buke V. Quickly and not sure if he saw. Wot
a cruel trick of fate that the glorious fudge-wigged
Basil should have the same initials as Brian Bolt,
prince of cardigans . . . Sure enuf, later, in the loos,
Aggy and Spiggy came in saying Brian's been
nagging them to ask me if I'll go out with him.

*Arg! Pictured above: a moment of innocence before
dread realization that the gorgeous fudge-wigged Basil
Barrington shares the same initials as Brian Bolt, Prince
of Cardigans...*

'Oh come off it. I don't think so. The one time we tried to kiss I cut my nose on his specs. No offence, but . . .'

Aggy took off her specs and started polishing them with the edge of my jumper. 'Look, he TOLD me to ask. That's all. So, will you?' she insisted.

'He makes me puke.'

'Oh, he's rather cute,' moons Aggy.

'When'd you last get your glasses checked? Come to that, when'd you last get your Nauseating Prat-o-Meter calibrated?'

'Well, anyway, he's really clever, he gets straight As in everything, just like me. I mean . . .' (she caught my beady eye) 'I'll shut up now.'

'C'mon Letty,' said Spiggy. 'Tell him you've got previous appointments for the rest of your life. Tell him you've got an incurable infectious disease that turns teenage boyz' private parts green . . . Tell him you're trying to break it to him gently, but he's a suppurating boil on the smirking face of the entire male gender, and soon it'll be no more Mizz Nice Gurl. Or just tell him NO THANKS.'

'Right,' I said. 'That part's easy. I'll just go now and tell him now no. No now.'

The others cheered.

I marched out straight into Brian. I hate it when boyz lurk about outside the gurlz' loos. It plays havoc with yr privacy. Come to think of it, the boyz wld be relieved not to have Ruth'n'Van'n'Elsie lurking about outside their toilets, as well. Anyway, was so

taken by surprise that found self smiling sheepish..
at Brian and being evasive. Out of the corner of my
eye I saw Spiggy shoot Aggy a 'what's the point'
look. Oh gawd. How have I done this again? Found
wimpy self telling Brian I'd go to the pix with him
on Sat.

Have decided that Spiggy and Spriggy are V. Well
suited. Jack Spriggs is a dead funny Jack-the-lad
type. He has drawn a picture of a little man on his
rubber. (OK, I know no one sez 'rubber' any more,
since we all found out it's American for condom, but
I can write it, can't I? Why should I write eraser? Eh?
Just cos Americans want to dominate whole werld,
yuniverse Etck?)

Today he produced a tiny doll's house armchair,
put it on his desk and sat the rubber in it. Even Ms
Farthing thought it was funny.

She was not so amused by poor old Priscilla Crump
turning up, to show off her
twins, though. P. Crump is
getting Home Tuition, but
I think she wld be better off
having full time army of
nannies, au pairs Etck as
dear little Rabina and Barin yell their little nuts off
non stop. Akshully, think the Farthing shld be
pleased about the visit as seeing the twins shld be an
excellent lesson in need for birth control, as Jack
pointed out.

Fri Jan 8

Elvis's birthday. He was born in 1935, so wld have been a bit ga ga by now even if he'd lived. However, lunies in his fan klub are alive and well and still believing he'll knock on their door luking as if he'd stepped straight out of Jail house Rock.

RE Assembly from Mr Portillo. I think pupils at Sluggs wld be V. Religious if they only had RE assemblies from Mr Ojungwe or Miss Applebright. But Portillo cld put off even the Archbish of Canterbury.

'As Jesus said, "the poor are always with you",' he droned. Well, the poor are certainly with him because Sluggs is hardly the kind of place where ye pupils fall out of convoys of Mercs, Rolls Royces, stretch limos every morning. Fall out of back doors of police vans more like. In his attempt to overcome ye 'natural disadvantages of his catchment area' Mr Portillo attempts to inject sense of enterprise and achievement in his charges.

He has a point in this. More kids live in poverty today than at any time since the 40s. This is V. Shocking fact. Groan-ups are always banging on about this stuff to demoralise poor Teenage Worriers, whose fault, I think, it is NOT.

But Portillo goes on to point out that the Good

Samaritan couldn't have helped anyone if he hadn't had any dosh. This is meant to encourage us to go out and Get Rich Quick so we can help others Etck. Some pupils at Sluggs already understand this. However, I have not noticed them crossing the road to offer recently acquired car radios, tellys Etck to poor unfortunates fallen by wayside.

Jesus wld turn in his cave at our Noble Headteacher's idea of Christian charity. However, though El Chubb has reluctantly to admit that 2000 years of ye doctrine of Lerve has not done all it might, I suspect that just encouraging the strongest to get rich and then maybe drop a few crumbs to the rest of us just leaves things the way they were.

Them and Us.

Was reminded of this forcibly today by poor old Svetlana Grutowski in tears. My first thort was that this crying thing is V. Contagious. I put it down to exam stress. But it turns out her brother in the Ukraine is having a hole-in-the-heart operation this week and the teddy she sent him has just got sent back as there was not enuf postage. Probably the same postman who stole Aggy's mother. Svetlana sez the surgeons in the Ukraine are paid about 5p a week and a loaf of bread costs 4p.

1 **am.** Have been trying to think of how to do my film. Must be something deep, true, soul searching. Must contrast War Zones with absurd privlidges of oiks like *moi*.

Overwhelmed with glumey midnite thorts: No call from Basil and the gharstly prospect of a date with Brian tomorrow. No doubt I will feel better in morning.

Sat Jan 9
BASIL COUNTDOWN: 21 DAYS

Woke up feeling as though have ten ton weight on hed. Surely glume not this bad? Panick at thort of poss brane tumour. But it was Rover, who had nested on my nut in her basket. I know she is only cat in werld who can open fridge, but how she drags a basket onto my nut is beyond *moi*.

Push Rover off only to confront thort-of-the-day: a date with Brian. How did I get self into this? Tonight, I will have to make it clear I do not want to see him again. The best way will be to say I lurve another. And I do. I do.

Hang out with Aggs and Hazel. Hazel sobbing over Mandy as usual. It's not exactly easy to nip up to Scotland for a cuddle. Aggs swotting in coffee bar as we talk.

'Don't you ever stop working? Hazel here has a problem.'

'Me too. Three little brothers, two little sisters and probably a dad to support.'

38

'Wot? Your dad's not losing his JOB?'

The poor *are* always with us. Aggy starts crying too.

I remember a far-off day when my mates were not always in tears. When we used to hang out and put chewing gum under people's coffee mugs in the local cafe Etck. Still, they are cheered up at thought of helping me get ready for gharstly date with Brian.

'We'll make you luke so hideous he'll run screaming out of the cinema.'

'Yeah. Shouldn't take long.'

Oh. Hah. hah.

We all trail back to my place and up into my apology for a bedrume. It's quite hard to fit all of us in, what with clothes, duvets, bean bags, soft toyz, Benjy's vehicles and my beloved rume being the size of an ant's loo in the first place. We pile onto the bed.

'Right. What you going to wear? How about this?' sez Aggy, picking up a gorilla mask of Benjy's and spifflicating herself with laughter. For a V. Brainy person, Aggy can sometimes be quite infantile.

'You could wear Rover as a scarf,' suggests Hazel. 'I heard Brian was very allergic.'

Rover not keen on this idea.

'Well. I dunno why you couldn't just tell old Brian to take a running jump,' says Hazel. 'Then Aggy could catch him on the way down.'

'Yeah. You could still say no,' volunteers Aggy hopefully, 'and I could go instead, and comfort him, and then engulf him in my voluptuous siren-like charms — er, arms.'

'Look, I know it was stoopid, but I felt sorry for him, right? I'll make it clear on the date that it won't work out.'

'Yeah yeah.'

Finally we decided on a simple outfit in various shades of soot, jet and midnight, which is all I have anyway . . .

I slunk off to the cinema early and armed *moi*self with jumbo popcorn and vast coke to give my mouth something to do that wouldn't involve Brian. Thought, hope it isn't going to be scary. Above all, mustn't bury head in his neck. The film, *I Was a Teenage Alien*, was a shlocky sci-fi romance in which the nerdy hero (dead spit of Brian, akshully, so hope this young actor doesn't get famous, which wld make Brian's hed even bigger) falls in love with a beautiful alien.

As the hero's arm snaked towards the alien, so Brian's arm snaked round *moi*. At this point I heard snickering, guffawing and disgusting popcorn chomping noises from the row behind. Aggs and Hazel had snuck in! Oh, very funny. And they are supposed to be my BFs . . .

Luckily, the beautiful alien reveals her true nature and slaps the hero with a tentacle.

I reveal my true nature and run for the Ladies, muttering 'Too much coke. Gonna be sick.'

Brian takes me home. I make fake puking gestures

all the way home and stagger into house leaving him forlorn on doorstep.

I am a coward, but am a very releeved coward.

Sun Jan 10
COOKING, GRANNY CHUBB
BASIL COUNTDOWN: 20 DAYS

London Underground opened Jan 10 1863. Fancy that. Wonder if they had Cockfosters station then? My dad's fave joke is V. Crowded train and someone shouting 'Is this Cockfosters?' and someone replying 'No, it's mine!' And they expect the younger generation to have good taste.

G. Chubb teaches me Yorkshire pudding. Hers is golden crispy fairy food but mine comes out luking like little lumps of coal. Why? We mixed it together and put it in the oven at the same time.

'Oh well, I'm sure it never works the first time,' she sez, kindly. Obviously you need elfin fingers, or elfin dust or something, and mine is just hobgoblin, or maybe ogre dust. Never mind, if I cannot be top chef in swanky restaurant. I can now cross that off my wish list along with ballerina and vet.

~~chef~~   fudge taster
~~ballerina~~   ~~vet~~

Story in local paper:

Mr Bert Scroggins of Arbuthnot Mansions, has threatened to sue the Prime Minister for an unjust and illegal war. Mr Scroggins said today:	*'I have always supported this government, but enough is enough. I have one son of eighteen and I am not going to sit by and see him called up to die.'*

There is never any point in thinking war is over for ever. Maybe Jesus shld have said, *War is always with you.*

Mon Jan 11
MATHS WORKSHOP
VILE EXAMS ALL DAY
BASIL COUNTDOWN: 19 DAYS

Science. Wrote about electricity as follows:

In about 600BC a Greek called Thales of Miletus discovered that if he rubbed a piece of amber with fur, the amber would pick up feathers. This was the first recorded discovery of static electricity.

If a body is highly charged in this way tiny particles of electricity, called electrons, may jump off it in the form of a spark, or even give a small electric shock.

About 1999 AD a Brit named El Chubb of Sluggs Comprehensive discovered that if Gurlz and Boyz rubbed themselves against each other sparks also flew, and they could pick up anything. This was a V. Recent discovery of static electricity and its relationship to STDs (er, sexually transmitted diseases).

Well. I thought it was qu good.

Thunderbolts, flashes of lightning, white hot heat Etck are all the language of Lurve and electricity between two people is indisputable to *moi*, since when I first saw Basil Barrington I felt as if I had plugged myself into the mains and lit up like a Christmas Tree. Akshully, if I cld make *moi*self look less like a Christmas Tree and more like a rose, or something, I might be able to pursue this New Relationship with elan. (**NB New Werd, Elan**. Meaning 'flair', but not applicable to bell bottom trousers.)

Tue Jan 12
VILE EXAMS ALL DAY
BASIL COUNTDOWN: 18 DAYS

Jack Spriggs bought in a little rocking chair for his rubber today. Said it had had a rough weekend.

Exam fever has hit Sluggs. There is an unearthly quiet as pupils struggle to skule having been up orl nite. Lots of caring, desperate parents have filled lunch boxes with hi-protein snax and hi-energy juice to juice up their addled Teenage Worriers for exams. Some addled Teenage Worriers are of course pepped up by all sorts of other, possibly less legal, substances, which they have taken the night before when trying to cram five years werk into 12 hrs, hence are asleep over their exam papers and must be constantly prodded to life by stern invigilator.

Have decided there is a WAY.

First, ask yr self: Have you got GCSE heeby-jeebies?
G-C-S-Es
are they:
Garstly **C**ataclysms **S**apping **E**nergy?
Do they put you in mind of:
Gum boils, **C**old sores, **S**uppurating **E**xcrescences?
Or:
Grisly **C**arbuncles **S**tretching **E**ndlessly?
Are they worth the:
Graft, **C**omas, **S**wotting, **E**ffort?
Well then. Take El Chubb's advice:
Go! **C**ry! **S**cream! **E**SCAPE!
Or, alternatively, read on . . .

Do you have a strange feeling that you may fail all of yr exams because, perhaps, you may not have always done yr homewerk on time?
Or at all?
Or that having a fag behind the bike shed made

you more *hereux* than going *Je ne fume pas, tu ne fume pas, il Elle et Nous ne fume pas?*

Moi of course will never fume anything, not after watching only parents gagging and hacking and coughing up greenish-black suppurating slimy mucus every morning, but don't let me put you off . . .

Is it possible you are not, after all, cut out to be the rocket scientist who will rescue Earthlings from the Incoming of the Inexorable Asteroid or the Designer-Label Dreamweaver who changes the style of a generation, but may end up behind the bar at the Dog & Duck? Or under the bar at the Dog & Duck?

If you answered 'Yes' to one or more of the above, do not despair.

It may surprise you that I, El Chubb, am fearless. I leap into the fray armed with a brand new fountain pen bought by Only Mother in vain attempt to make my handwriting less like a walrus ink-dancing with a spider, and tell *moi*self: I have done my werst, there is no hope.

So why Worry? I can take whotever the cruel examiners throw at *moi*. However, I do not boast, not I.

Not like boffin Chlamydia Clutterbuck. 'Hey wasn't that easy-peasy?' she pukily proclaims after each exam, wondering why everyone pours their hi-energy juice down her bra.

Most agonized Teenage Worriers think: if only I could get the exam papers. They plot and toil and try to bribe their teachers Etck, to no avail. Svetlana's cousin's frend's dad works at a printers who akshully print exam papers! But he is kept gagged and trussed in a dungeon for five months before the exams. Even so, the truth, dear fellowe sufferers, is that even if you had the exam questions, you wld have to werk V. Hard to get the answers right.

No. That is not The Way.

I have a better idea. I am currently patenting the Chubb-Aggy-time-nodule (sorry, module) which will propel the Chosen few (that is, me and my frendz) into the Future, not to get the questions, but to get all the highest marked *answers*. Time wld stand still in the classrume, which wld allow us to arse about in the future, copying answers out in all sorts of handwriting with wel chosen speling mistakes Etck. Then we cld flog them to the whole class for large dosh, also helping local community by putting Sluggs ahead of St Cheynganggs in ye dread league tables. I can see the local paper now:

HURRAH FOR SLUGGS!

Best comprehensive in Werld! The boyz and gurlz of Sluggs comp have shown the playing fields of Eaten a thing or two. 100% have A* GCSEs. Headmaster Mr Portillo said today: 'A combination of a caring sharing environment, skule uniform and a plentiful supply of india rubbers has put Sluggs up there at the cutting edge with the movers and shakers.'

46

Of course, even this plan cld backfire, as you wld still have to match the answers to the questions and I can imagine many people in humble Sluggs saying how grately they admire the philosopher Picasso, the exquisite embroidery of Mozart and the stunning symphonies of W. Shakespeare. As for Einstein's theory of evolution and Darwin's brill stuff on why your relatives, travelling in opposite directions at fantastick speeds, will always get together again at Christmas to remind each other that they never sent a postcard from the place where the universe bends. Well, kool.

But I am sure Aggs and I will have werked out this time travel thing and ironed out any little glitches by the time of the real exams. If you want one, just send a cheque for £80 million pounds/ecus/dollars to El Chubb, c/o my publishers. Ta.

Tried to find something interesting to say about Hamlet.

Now Hamlet is a V. V. Interesting subject, but it's funny how uninteresting it can seem when you're desperately trying to drag together every halfbaked scrap of information you can, in the hope that some eville examiner from the Spanish Inquisition will be fooled into thinking you are werthy of that Passport to Proper Persondom which is a GCSE.

Ah, there's the rub, as Hamlet said on his way to the massage parlour. I bet Hamlet never so much as sat a single GCSE. If he had, he would have learned the benefits of hard werk, the identifying of clear goals Etck, the ability to marshal hard info without emotional diversions and all this.

Gadzooks Etck!

Mother de-nitted Benjy today.

'I got 24 nits,' he proudly said, showing me a tissue

littered with little ded headlice. I draw the line at feeling sorrow for these useless creatures. Wot good do they do werld?

'Letty, you must do your hair. It says clearly, everyone in the family must . . .'

Sit with disgusting nit stuff on hed for hours. Imagine Shakespearian nit-drama as little strutting and fretting nits act out their pathetick hopes and dreams before the gods rain down eville nit-destroying monsoon on them.

Me and Benjy in Shakespearian NIT drama: "As nits to wanton boyz are we to Pharmacists..." Etck

Hed still itching.

Nobody phones.

Life is just great. Exams, no frendz, no boyfrend, nits.

Wed Jan 13
BABYSIT

VILE EXAMS ALL DAY

BASIL COUNTDOWN: 17 DAYS

Today, there were 28 little rubbers altogether. Sunil has bought in four: a pink one, a blobby putty one, an ordinary bog standard one and one like Mickey Mouse. He has made a wizard's hat for one of them. The playmobile chairs and sofas and hammocks are cluttering up the desks. Vesta Currie (I know, I know, but that is her name, I suppose Mr and Mrs Currie thort it wld be a bit of a laarf) has bought in an entire three piece doll's house suite, decorated in Balham Gothic orange and purple swirls. Zelda has got the wrong end of the stick as usual and bought in a quite big rubber ball, which she attempted to place in Siegfried the crazed Science master's trousers. Her helper has to take her outside for exams, which is good. It stops her playing with my hair and whistling the *Titanic* theme tune.

4.30 pm. At last! Postcard from Basil! Whoopee!

Not V. Interesting even *moi* has to admit. Will I pick up a parcel for him from the post office.

Well, it's not exactly the earth moving, but it's something.

Thur Jan 14
VILE EXAMS ALL DAY
BASIL COUNTDOWN: 16 DAYS

Jack Spriggs bought in a tuna can lined with blue stickyback. He filled it with water and kept plopping his rubber into it.

'Erasers never get any breaks. So I thought I'd make 'im a swimming pool.'

Could not concentrate on Vile exams due to Benjy's nightmare about cork tiles. He came into my rume three times last night. The third time he said he wasn't scared any more but he couldn't go to sleep because he couldn't decide which eyelid to shut first.

Basil's parcel had already been returned to sender but at least I tried.

Fri Jan 15

FREEDOM! Exam-free paradise. Tiddley dee!

Jack Spriggs added a little diving board to his tuna tin swimming complex. Ms Farthing said a joke was a joke and no-one had a better sense of humour than she, but was he going to build an entire aqua-park and if so where would he put his werk?

'Aqua park. Nice idea, mate,' said Spriggy.

'I am not your mate, I am your teacher,' replied the icy Farthing. Next thing, rubbers will be forbidden, which will be fun cos we can all use spit and fingers tearing holes in the paper Etck just like in olden days, shortly before being executed by cruelle headmaster Etck.

We have a project to keep us keen until the real exams . . . we are supposed to write to a penfriend somewhere. We had to pick them out of a hat.

I got China. This is V. Exciting. Apparently Lotus can write V. Good English, so I luckily don't have to learn Chinese which wld be hard since even a sentence of Chinese writing looks like the wall of an art gallery. Maybe I will get to visit and go on Grate Wall Etck. One-party state, slaughter of Chinese students are possible probs but I don't want to get her into trouble.

Can't wait to tell Alfonsa about my film idea.
    What shld I call it? Can't be *War & Peace*. Have
scoured skule library for lists of war bukes, but
they are all called something totally weird, like
Birdsong, or *Regeneration* which just sound like BBC
nachur progs.

I haven't told anyone else what Josef said about the
barber. It's burning a hole in my brain.

11 pm. Film course was totaly excellente. Alfonsa
loves my idea. Sez I shld interview some of the boyz
on the film course and that she can rent a video
camera to me V. Cheap from next week, if I can pay
her at the end of term. Right then. I will have to
bite bullet and do paper round.

Sat Jan 16
BASIL COUNTDOWN: 14 DAYS

Aggy rang first thing, in floods. She has been
robbed.
    Well, her whole flat, akshully.
    This is really bad news. Aggy's whole family
went out (they never go out) for a pizza to celebrate
Aggy's dad's birthday — and also, as it happens, to
take his mind off the fact that it was on his

birthday that Aggy's mum ran off with the postman, how could she? And, when they got back, the place was ransacked.

The telly, the anciente water-powered computer with the abacus-based superchip that Agg's dad found in a skip, Mandarin's life savings (Mandarin is six and had saved £3.78p to run away with), £20 that Aggs's dad kept for emergencies. This is a living nightmare. Aggs' dad threatened with redundancy, her mum off stretching the envelope in the arms of the postman. Arg. Wot can I do to help? Wot? Wot?

Go straight round and find place swarming with cops like the Bill. Well, not exactly swarming. One rather knackered-looking officer patiently taking down list of missing objects.

'An' they've taken my penknife.'

'An' my Crash Bundicoot.'

Horrible. Fancy stealing from little kids.

Aggy is really really upset about one thing: a silver charm bracelet that her mum gave her when she was born. She has been adding a charm to it every year.

'I was going to get a silver mushroom this year,' she sobbed. I *think* she said 'mushroom'.

My mum was V. Sorry about the burglary but V. Unsympathetic when I went on about Aggy's mum and the postman, and just said, good for her, grate that a woman in her forties can find happiness when all she's done is look after about forty kids for 20 years.

How can my Only Mother be so cruel? Aggy's dad is the nicest, most caring man in werld.

Sun Jan 17
COOKING, GRANNY CHUBB
BASIL COUNTDOWN: 13 DAYS

Do mushroom pizza and take it round to Aggs's family. There is only enuf for V. Small slice each. But it is the thort that counts. When I say it is mushroom, Aggs gulps and sniffs. Must've been a silver mushroom then. Thinks: every person is an island; do I even really know my Best frendz?? Aggy's dad, who has always been so V. Kind, caring, sharing, and a rock-of-ages Etck now lukes like he is suffering the shock of ages which he is.

Sit up into nite making lists of boyz to interview. S'pose I'll have to do creeps like Brian and werse creeps like Syd Snoggs to get full picture. Maybe there will be a budding anti-war poet among them? On to fame and forchune, I mean on to werthy role as visionary discoverer of poetick diamonds in the rough Etck.

Mon Jan 18
Martin Luther King Day, USA
MATHS WORKSHOP
BASIL COUNTDOWN: 12 DAYS

! Interesting Fact: Scott of the Antarctic reached South Pole on Jan 18 1922.

'It has come to my attention,' said Mr Portillo, 'that certain individuals – I name no names – have been behaving very childishly with their equipment. I would like to point out that pencils are utensils used for writing. And that rubbers are utensils used for rubbing out the many mistakes you are likely to make on your journey through life. I would hate to be forced to confiscate such precious items.'

There you go. You read it here first. They'll confiscate pencils next. We'll have to scratch on slates like our grandparents.

He then moved on to ponder the legacy of the late great black civil rights leader Martin Luther King, whose day this is.

Did not think it was possible to make Martin – 'I have a Dream' – Luther King sound boring, but Portillo managed it with ease. Fortunately this did not apply to our V. Excellent RE teacher Mr Ojungwe, who didn't go on and on about him but just played us a recording of the 'I have a Dream' speech which left even the most wired and twitchily macho of the Boyz in my class silent and amazed.

Martin Luther King has to be one of the wickedest speechifyers ever, and able to inspire the peeples of the werld to believe in a Better Life.

This will help with my film too, sez El Chubb selfishly, (and therefore not in keeping with spirit of 'I Have A Dream' speech), but I Have A Dream Too and you have to start somewhere. I may even cut some of the speech into the movie.

I also do Have a Dream where my dear brainy Aggy will be prime minister and the werld will be pure and free of strife. Huh.

Zelda was playing with my hair for about five hours today. She either plays with your hair or twirls about being Rose in *Titanic*. She is away with the fairies. Luckily her helper has V. Long hair that she doesn't mind having lots of V. Small plaits and tangles in.

Am doing first interview with Boy after skule. Have asked Sunil's brother, Raj, as he is V. Nice and quiet and will not make me nervous.

Also he is 19, so if the Current Situation escalates, or if ever the werld went to the brink again, the army would be after him like a shot, offering him a once-only chance to travel and meet other young people with similar interests, ie: fear and hoping to shoot first.

V. Odd to think that all American men my dad's age had to fight in Vietnam (with some exceptions like the odd president and other blokes rich enuf to buy their way out or skive off to other countries Etck). Not that I blame them. Wld draw line *moi*self at equal rights for gurlz to get mown down in war Etck. Apparently women behave much better in war zones than men, becoming caring sharing people and not behaving irrationally according to Mum, who said she'd much rather have a woman than a bloke beside her in the trenches so to speak.

Unfortunately, Raj V. Quiet during interview.

When I reran the tape, all I could hear was 'er . . .' and 'um' and a lot of clattering cutlery. Maybe Cholesterol Charlie's Cafe is not the best place to do an interview . . .

Must improve questioning technique. Will practise on Benjy, who may tragickly be one of next generation of victims. Who knows?

Spend evening writing to Lotus. Enclose most flattering photo of self that I can find. Tell her it is V. Bad one. Takes ages to copy out Chinese address.

Tue Jan 19
BASIL COUNTDOWN: 11 DAYS

Practise interviewing techniques on Benjy. Viz:

'What would you think if all the little boyz in your class were asked to go and fight in a real war?'

'Not big enough.'

'Well, not just the small ones. ALL the boys in your class.'

'Me too?'

'Yes. You too.' (gulp)

'Would we get guns?'

'Yes.'

'Real AK47s an' revolvers, an' Uzis and Walther PPKs?'

'Yes.'

'Wiv bullets?'

'Yes.'

(Are all interviews like this? They must have to cut big chunks out of them when they show them on telly . . .)

'Real bullets?'

'Yes.'

'KOOL.' (pause) 'An' would we get light sabres?'

'Er, no, probably not light sabres.'

'That's not FAIR.'

'Yes, but Benjy, what would you do?'

'WIN.'

'No, but really, Benjy, would you like to be in a

59

REAL war, you know, with real people getting killed?'

'Who?'

'Who what?'

'Who would get killed?'

'Well, maybe anyone, maybe everyone.'

'Would Mrs Hambottom get killed?'

'Maybe.'

'Good.'

'But I might get killed. Or . . .' (casting about desperately) 'or Horace, or Kitty . . .'

'No. I'd save them.'

'But supposing you couldn't?'

Benjy burst into tears. I think he is too young to understand this stuff. I read somewhere that the age of reason is seven, but it may come a bit later than that in Benjy's case.

Wed Jan 20
BABYSIT
BASIL COUNTDOWN: 10 DAYS

Card from Basil. Sez he's OK and longs to see *moi*. Hooray. Wants me to pick up another parcel. Boo. Hope I have more success with this than larst one. Still, maybe it's not so bad to be somebody's humble servant if you and the somebody lerve each other selflessly. Not sure if this is the case yet, but have hopes.

Take Basil's card round to Aggy, to read for tell-tale signs. Aggy puts on her best Professor manner.

'Hmm. "Darling" – a bit forward for someone who's only met you at a party for about three seconds.'

'But, Aggs, I know I didn't meet him face to face, but you KNOW we talked masses on the phone last year and he helped me get over Adam.'

'True. True. But still "missing you madly", bit over-the-top? Eh?'

'OK. You're trying to tell me he has a girlfriend. You've talked to Junior. Go on. I can take it.'

'No. I haven't. I've been a bit busy. You know, Dad's job, burglaries, GCSEs . . . little distractions like that.'

'Aggs. Please. Please phone him. Please phone him now.'

She relents. But Basil's flatmate, big kind hunky Junior, is out.

'Look, I will. Promise.'

'Aggs, you are the Best.'

Aggs is the best. But there are still no leads on the robbers. The police have only been back in touch once since it happened. Is this wot we pay our taxes for? Etck. Maybe I could get a job as private detective solving all unsolved crimes. I will start with Aggs.

'Aggy. I will solve this crime. I will interview all your neighbours. Someone is bound to have seen something.'

'I think,' said Aggy wearily, 'the police have probably done that.'

But I am not so sure.

On the way out of Aggy's block of flats, I bump into an old lady who lives on the ground floor.

'Have the police asked you about the robbery?' I ask.

She scampers into her flat and I hear the clanging of two thousands bolts. Hmm. Must be more subtle. Perhaps the way to interview people about crime is to start: 'Hello. You've won the Lottery. To qualify, you need to answer a few simple questions.'

Go to post office on way back. No parcel. I am a failure. I cannot even pick up a parcel.

Thur Jan 21
BASIL COUNTDOWN: 9 DAYS

Rain, nothing happens.

Fri Jan 22
FILM COURSE
BASIL COUNTDOWN: EIGHT DAYS

Interesting Fact: Battle of Rorke's Drift, as celebrated in fab film Zulu fought on this day in 1879. Zulu is famous for having a scene where a little red post office van is driving along the desert horizon, thus proving it was filmed on Clapham Common or somewhere, but I can't say I've ever spotted it. Too busy admiring nice peaceful forgiving Zulus.

Excellente film course. *Tout le monde tres* impressed with my idea.

'Purrfect theeng for ze new millenium,' purrs Alfonsa as all the males in rume sag at knees and foam at mouth. I do like Alfonsa but think she is a little overabundant in the cleavage dept. However, must admit she has good taste. I admire her view of my creative skills enormously. 'Yourrr feelm,' she continues, 'eeees telling tchrooo nachure of ze warrr culchure of ze male which 'as become so powerful in zees larst century zat more people 'ave died zees way zan in ze 'ole 'istory of ze 'uman race before eet. Eeeef women were to run zeee werld, would zey go arrround bloweeeeeng up ze leeeeedle babeeeees?'

'No, no,' we chorus. Wrong.

'Don't be so naeeeeeeeeve,' she snaps. 'EEEEt is powerrr, not genderrr, zat eees ze prrobleme. You can bet your dollere's bottom' (I think she meant to say 'bottom dollar') 'that eeef women 'ad ze power, zey would use it just like ze men. Look at Meeseeze Thatchere.'

Some of us, like *moi*, were still in nappies when the notorious Mrs Thatcher ruled this once Grate Nation. But we have heard about her, of course. My dear Only Father bangs on about little else. Sez her idea that there is No Such Thing as Society sent us all back to the Dark Ages.

Hmmm. Not sure Alfonsa's right, though. I mean, all the gurlz I know don't run around with guns as much as boyz and they don't fight as much either. Except Syd Snoggs's sisters, and Van, Ruth and Elsie's gang.

Wonder if cld turn film into V. Insightful Battle of Sexes type thingy, but don't trust El Chubb branepower enough, so feel it's prob safer to let my film speak for itself. And it's time boyz got to say wot they think insted of just obediently going off as cannon fodder. Maybe loads of them will say they hate war, anyway.

'Can I be interviewed for your film?' said small quiet round Stanley. We were all startled since this is the longest sentence Stanley has ever spoken.

'Of course, Stanley,' I say encouragingly. 'And anyone else who would like to . . .'

There is an embarrassing silence. Either all the other blokes are scared of revealing their latent bloodlust on film, or they are jealous of my brilliant ideaz. Alfonsa whips them into shape, however, and soon I have a line up of: Stanley, Kurt Flasher, Bageshott Hardy (still wrestling with his murder-mystery-whodunnit) and a long thin streak of a bloke dressed entirely in pale pink, so he looks like a Smartie that got sent to the liquorice factory by mistake. His name is Saul Spangle, so he's probably in a band. Kurt has abandoned his project on British Waterways for a film about the power struggles in a pub darts team, oh good, that will be more interesting then. I make dates to interview them all and go home on wings of song.

My film is nearly finished! It will make itself!

NB New werd: naeeeeeeeeve, as Alfonsa called it, is akshully spelt 'naive' and means innocent, or 'unconsciously and amusingly simple'. Stupid, in other werds, like *moi*.

Will Dad-racing ever make it on to *Eurotrash*?

Cozy evening with Indian take-away, watching TV.

Oh, hurray, Snail racing on Eurotrash. You race them along trails of wine. If it were Old Bastard lager this wld suit Dad. The winner is returned to the wild (if that's where snails live) and the losers are eaten. Just like life.

Sat Jan 23

To give Mum a Birthday Treat, decide to clear out Benjy's rume.

Aggy helped me move all of the furniture (well, a bed, a chair and a chest of drawers) out of Benjy's rume, in vain attempt to cure his floor phobia. His little bed, painted with a dinky Bambi, was surprisingly heavy until we discovered he had been sleeping with eight of Dad's old encyclopaedias.

'In case I wake up and want to know sumfink.'

'But Benjy, you can hardly read *Teddy Goes to the Slot Machine.*'

When we finally got the carpet up we realized why Benjy's convinced it's a swamp/whirlpool/kwicksand Etck. He has been living on top of layers of Lego, playmobile, soft toys, chewing gum, bath sponges, towels, old socks.

'How did all this stuff get under here?' asked Aggy, innocently.

'PUT it back, I like it!' screamed Benjy. 'It there to make floor cosy.'

'But it will be much nicer when it's all smooth,' I assure him.

'No NO NO! The floor wants it. Will eat ME otherwise,' he shouts.

I see. To placate the floor gods he has been making sacrifices.

We tried to clean the carpet. It is quite a nice soft mushroom colour akshully, but I rubbed a corner with dabitoff and discovered a rather loud sky blue lurks a few layers beneath the surface.

'Ooh, look, Benjy, it's a lovely blue.'

'No NO NO. Want mushroom. Mushroom is cuddly.'

Aggy looked dreamy. She was thinking of her silver mushroom I suppose. In the end we gave in and put everything back.

So much for keeping resolutions.

Father is pushing the boat out and taking us all to the posh Chinese for Only Mother's birthday.

'Oh, Leonard. But you'll miss The Book Thingy,' said Mum, blushing.

'I'll tape it,' sez Dad, merrily.

It is V. Nice of Dad to be prepared to miss big posh interview on telly with his anti-hero, Frank LeSpeaking, who wrote a heart-rending account of his impoverished childhood, made about five million dollars out of it and went into therapy. I've got to hand it to Dad. He may be really jealous of the fact that his own star has waned, but he does show other writers respect. He'd be great up there talking to Melvyn Bragg Etck about his struggles to find food for his young siblings and making a crust of bread last all day by tearing it into little pieces, sucking it, drying it over a crackling match for later Etck. Also, he does stick by us, sort of. I think.

Have made mother V. Nice birthday card. But of course it is Benjy's old rubbidge that gets all the attention. He has made something involving milk bottle tops and a not V. Well-washed yoghurt carton and some wool. It is supposed to be a 'sculpture' of Mum. From the attention it gets, you'd think it was by Michelangelo, at least.

At Foo-King's we push the boat out. It is the poshest Chinese for miles, but is quite unpleasant inside, V. Pale greenish lights with those blurry pictures of waterfalls that are supposed to look like they move but make your eyes go funny if you look at them too long. Worst thing, from Benjy's point of view, no burgers, no chips.

'Come on, Benjy, try some Chinese, it's lovely.'

Parents always say this about food-u-hate. When you are two, they push vast sprout at you. They forget that to your little eyes the sprout is the size of a cauliflower. 'Come on. It's lovely,' they say. No, it is not. It tastes like frog's farts. You know that, and more sinisterly, *they know it too*. Thus, the fragile bond of trust twixt infant and parent is broken.

Course, I am above all that and relish the old chicken and cashew, spring rolls, duck'n'pancake Etck. But persuading Benjy takes most of the evening. He finally tries a little duck, before going: 'No. No. Fed it yesterday.'

'Ate it yesterday darling. No, you didn't, you haven't tried duck before.'

'No. Fed it. Yesterday, in park.'

'Oh. Ah. No, no. This is a Chinese duck.'

Benjy compromises by scoffing six Spring rolls (poor little innocent Springs, poor little helpless rolls . . .).

Dad sticks a candle in the lychee and we sing Happy Birthday. But I keep wanting to go home, cos of thinking of Aggs going out for her dad's birthday and then getting home to robbed house. Feel panick-stricken that same thing will have happened to us. Maybe shld never go out . . . Hope am not becoming neurotick.

Home to find house not robbed and video not working.

'Effword effword stupid technology,' snarls raging bull Father. 'Now I can't see what that effword tosser said about his new effword tossing book.'

Mother puts hand over Benjy's ears and raises eyes heavenward in sainted martyr luke she reserves for such occasions. Benjy is sick on her nice dress. The revenge of the Spring Rolls.

'A perfect end to a perfect day,' she murmurs.

2 am. Woke up from dream where I went out to interview boy for film but found self interviewing Brussels sprout, instead:

Moi: Your leaves look very crisp - have you washed the weevils out?

Brussels sprout: How kind, but I'm having a bad leaves day.

Moi: No. They look a lovely bright green, really. Good shine. Almost tasty. Um, if you like sprouts that is, I mean . . .

Brussels sprout: No worries, I'm used to it. First the compliments, then the saucepan. Then, LEFT - All alone on the side of the plate. How would YOU like it? If only I were a carrot (sob).

Moi: Oh, I don't know, carrots aren't so hot . . .

Brussels sprout: Some of them are no better than they should be. But I'd give anything for those lovely jackets the potatoes are wearing this season . . .

Moi: (panicking that interview not Deep and Meaningful enuf): Er, what do you think of vegetarianism as such.

Brussels sprout: No comment

At this point, the Brussels sprout metamorphosed magickly into Bart Simpson saying 'Eat My Shorts.'

Maybe that's what Teenage Worriers with eating disorders will end up doing:

MENU

Toasted Trainers
Pants Parfait
Sauteed Sweatshirt
Vest vol au Vent
Socks in chocolate

Sun Jan 24
COOKING, GRANNY CHUBB
BASIL COUNTDOWN: SIX DAYS

Interesting Fact: Gold first discovered in California, Jan 24 1848. This led to Gold Rush, decimation (NB New werd, usually used to mean destruction, but actually meaning killing one in ten) of Indians, and, ultimately, Mickey Mouse and McDonalds.

Hang out with Aggs and Hazel.

Things are not looking up in either dept.

Hazel is moping badly after Mandy and in despair about her posh skule. At St Cheynganggs, they all have to do five hours homework every night and unless you are in the top 4% of 'high achievers' the teachers laugh at you, cut you ded in the corridor, superglue dunce's hat to yr nut Etck. Hazel also has a two-hour journey each way. Sometimes I wonder whether it is really werth parents paying out a fortune to torture their kiddies in private skules. In Hazel's sex education lessons, no-one even mentions the Possibility of being gay, and their worst insult is 'lezzie'. It's like the dark ages. It makes old Sluggs luke like a Haven of Ye Enlightenment Etck. At least at old Sluggs there is a bit of community spirit Etck.

Werst of all, at Cheynganggs poor old Hazel has to wear a straw hat (they call them 'boaters', perluke!). Hazel stuffs hers in her pocket to avoid

71

Ruth'n'Van'n'Elsie's gang who lurk by the bus stop showing their knickers to boyz and baiting the posh girls on their way home. (Trouble is, when Hazel puts her boater on again it lukes like it's been sat on by an elephant.)

A typical exchange, Hazel sez, goes like this:

'Ullo. Hazel. Ooh, look, it's old Hazel, wot used to be in Crumbs Infants and then went up to the posh school.'

'Oooh Yeah. Hazel. Wasn't it Hazel who used to wet her knickers lunchtimes and get taken home by a NANNY?'

'Oh. Yeah. Great to see you, Hazel. How yer doin'?'

'Fine, thank you.'

'How's life up the manor house?'

'Fine, thank you.'

'Can we try on yerrat?'

'No, thank you.'

'Oh go on, Haze, let's have a go, oooh, does my brain look big in this?'

And so on.

Aggs has cheered up V. Slightly as her dad has another year's contract. He's an under-manager at FATS. Apparently, a few years ago, he would have had this job for life, which sounds like a prison sentence to *moi* but which is obviously V. Imp to adults hoping to keep their families from starvation, glume, long boring arguments about Keeping Hed Above Water Etck. This is one of the things Mrs Thatcher put a stop to, I gather. Now everyone has a yearly contract if they are V. V. Lucky and if you are over 45 they swap it over for a discount funeral at an undertaker's of your choice, 20% off if you use it in the next five years.

My Only Father goes ballistick when he hears about the treatment of Aggs's dad. In the olden days, he sez, when Trades Unions supported humble workers and there were quaint olde fashioned notions like Ye Job Securitye, Ye Sicke leave, Ye Holidaye Paye, Ye Strike On Ye Feebleste Pretexte Etck, workers used to stick their finger up at bosses behind their backs and sit around moaning about the state of the nation, lack of dosh Etck. Now, if you are lucky enough to get a short-term contract of any kind (which means they will guarantee your money at least until next payday), you have to run around like lemming, suck up to boss like mad, tell him/her you wld cross volcanoes ice floes Etck for chance to sit at their desk helping them make money till Dumesday, helping them sack less efficient werkers Etck.

'But is it werth it?' asks my poor poverty-stricken father. 'Is it good for people to be either working such long hours so they never see their family OR to be out of work making their family and frendz miserable by wailing, gnashing, mooning about and nicking car radios?'

I try to maintain a tactful silence as wld sometimes secretly prefer my Only Father to be Big Thrusting Daddy with Big Thrusting Wallet and no time to nag *moi*.

Anyway, Aggy's dad was saved by the only manager at FATS who has a passing resemblance to a human bean and knows how many kids Aggs's Dad has to support and took pity on him. But where will Aggs's dad be next year, if that boss leaves?

1 am. Woken by dreade thort that War creates jobz. Lots of luvley jobz making bombz, gunz, bulletz, uniforms Etck Etck. Lots of lovely jobz fighting. Lots of people killed so more jobz for those left behind. Arg. Must werk this into many themes of film.

1.10 am. Why can't I just make nice soppy romance about Teenage Lurve?

1.20 am. Maybe cld make loads of dosh with lurve story and then use dosh to Stop War?

2 am. Voice of Josef eating into brane . . .

Mon Jan 25
BASIL COUNDOWN: 5 DAYS

6 am. Woke up to find self entwined with Benjy, Elly, Bogey, Fartles and Rover.
'Benjy,' I croak sweetly. 'I love it when you come to share your sleeplessness with me. But please leave Elly or Bogey or Fartles behind. This bed ain't big enough for the five of us.'

'What's Basil?' asks Benjy in most charming tones.

'A herb,' I say with lightning speed of forked lightning. 'Why?'

'Must be a very NICE herb,' sez Benjy.

Oh no. Sleeptalking. Next it will be sleepwalking and I will embarrass self by turning up at Basil's at 3 am naked except for flannelette nightie. Decide to get slinky nightwear, just in case. Colder though. Will NOT give up bed socks, however. Not till May.

Unheard of: Akshully had interesting history lesson. In American studies we did some stuff on Calamity Jane. Was surprised by this for several reasons. Have seen various replicas of Calamity Jane on TV Etck, and she always seems to be galloping round and round a circus ring going 'yee-haw!' and firing blank bullets at pyramids of tin cans somebody knocks down from behind a second too late.

But the real Calamity Jane turns out to be something else.

Usually, all Western type movies of this period are about Lean, Gritty Etck white heroes who shoot about seven million Greasy, Indian Cliches, Destroy A Village In Order to Save It Etck. The only Gurlz you see in these films are doing all the washing, cooking, whoring, screaming Etck. BUT Calamity Jane was a real live Lean, Gritty Etck Female Heroine from those times who had wild times with famous lawman Wild Bill Hiccup.

As usually happens in the US of A, they don't

think Real Life is anything like as good as Entertainment, so Calamity Jane started doing stuff for paying audiences, appearing in Wild West Shows Etck. Sadly, she was fired for drunkenness, and thus must have been about the only drunk in the Wild West to have lost a job for this reason.

Haven't had so much fun in History since we did the Spanish Inquisition and all the boyz tortured their little rubbers (Oh, all right then, erasers) Etck.

But wonder, shld I turn my film into modern Western? Syd Snoggs as black-hatted thug, Brian as nerdy sheriff, Basil as white-hatted rescuer on palomino stallion with lasso (swoon). And *moi*, as magnificent Apache chieftain, galloping up at last minute on my Appaloosa mare and revealing I am a woman chief and need the lurve of a gude man Etck.

Maybe not. V. Old movies Adored Father likes have all these easily identifiable signs and symbols in them but it's all got V. Confusing lately. The Good Guys Dress In Black, Remember That.

Tue Jan 26
Australia Day
PERIOD DUE
MATHS WORKSHOP (COR, WOT A COMBINATION)
BASIL COUNTDOWN: 4 DAYS

Period arrives on time like vast ocean. Am V. Fond of Ozzie mates Spiggy and Dot, but do not feel urge to celebrate Australia Day. Feel this cld be due to Ruth'n'Van'n'Elsie charging round playground with lethal boomerang, saying 'show us yer willy, cobber' to any poor unsuspecting boy who is unfortunate enuf to cross their path.

Maybe gurlz *are* getting tougher than boyz?

I sit on bench with Aggs, clutching stomach and moaning soft moan. Have read about women 'keening' when in pain and grief.

'Woss up wiv you Letty? Got the painters in?'

'No, her Prince has come,' says Aggy, in poncey swottish tone.

'Eh?' sez I.

'That's what they said in the seventeenth century,' replies Aggy.

Well fancy that. I can't stand all these stoopid euphemisms like 'monthlies' (ooh, is that a new magazine, then?), 'curse' (mediaeval witches – shock horror), 'woman's troubles' (peryuke) and, 'It's That Time of the Month' (muttered in dark tones and capital letters by your mother to her frend when all you are doing is a bit of perfectly reasonable shouting). Let's just go for it. All together now:

'No, I haven't got the bloody painters in, I've got a bloody PERIOD, OK?'

'Ooh. Real,' sneers Ruth.

But good, good news. Basil has not got a gurlfrend. Official.

Tra li la li la.
Skippedy doo.
Tiddley plumpetty
sky is bloooooooooooo.

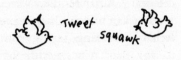
Tweet squawk

Periods don't affect mude, tra la.
Not if your mude is gude, tra la.
They make bad mude werse, tiddley pom
that's the end of my verse, tiddley pom.

L. Chubb discovery: When mude is gude, periods make no difference! Skippetty wippetty.

11 pm. Must admit though, am feeling a little low, considering wonderful news re Basil Etck.
Maybe Josef?
Or period?

Wed Jan 27
Holocaust Memorial Day
Babysit
Basil Countdown: 3 Days

Interesting Fact: Telly started today! On Jan 27 1926 John Logi Baird first demonstrated TV. Let us all thank John Logi, from the heart of our bottoms, for the Simpsons. **!**

2 am. Father has just woken us all up cos he's seen a

meteor. Adored Mother Worried it might be DTs, where too much alcohol makes you see things that aren't there. Benjy comes wailing to my bed. He now thinks what's Up There could be at least as scary as what's Down There, and since there's a lot more sky than floors this could be the start of a whole new werld of Misery and Glume for him.

Skule assembly on National Holocaust Day. Also the anniversary of the liberation of Auschwitz and, though we've seen bitz of this on film before, screening of historic newsreels left us all reeling in horror . . .

Feel pathetick at worries over Insignificant thingz like spotz and boyz . . .

Feel determined to pursue film-making career too after this proof of power of dockumentary record . . .

8 pm. Another card from Basil. He must be my boyfriend.

Darling Letty,
I saw a flamingo today and thought of
you. So graceful. Could you be an angel
(well, you are already) and phone Sam
for me and just say the parcel will be in
a hole in a wall at a multi-storey
carpark in Wapping, Saturday, 11.15.
Thanks a MILLION.
Love,
Baz

x x x x

The amazing Ms Chubb,
Heartbreak Hovel,
Codswallop,
UK

Baz! There's hip for you. Sounds like a DJ. Have feeling he made that remark about me being an angel already before. No, not a feeling, in fact, a certainty, as previous postcard etched into brane. Still, he loves me, else why wld he bother with such flattery? Not sure about the flamingo, though. Hope not reference to vast beak and tendency to flap.

Left message for Sam on ansaphone. Dunno why he can't just get parcels like everyone else, but then Baz moves in mysterious ways. Remember assembly, and hope flares up: if Baz and *moi* can werk together in future, maybe horrors like that wld never happen again . . .

Thur Jan 28
BASIL COUNTDOWN: 2 DAYS

Ruth'n'Van'n'Elsie are on my case.

'How's yor mate Hazel, nowot I mean? Too good for us, Eh?'

At least they only think Hazel's posh and are probably jealous of her stunning looks, grace, loads of dosh Etck. I can't help thinking, if Hazel were to Come Out and say she loves a gurl, then it wld be better if she changed her bus route . . .

Try to find quiet corner to have lunch alone with Aggy, but Ruth'n'Van'n'Elsie come and plonk themselves down next to us and talk V. Loudly about sex.

I don't like to admit this, but me and Aggs had our ears out on stalks.

'Har har har. He NEVER,' smirked Ruth'n'Elsie.

'Did he have a big one?' asked Ruth.

Van thought. 'Well I thought e'd got a milkbottle stuck in his jeans feraminnit, Nowotimean?' Har har har. 'Wot YOU looking AT?' She turned and snarled at us. 'Ain't you never seen a willy?'

Aggs and me, blushing from the roots of our roots, made our excuses and left.

'They're disgusting,' said Aggs.

'I know. But have you?'

'Have I what?'

'You know, seen a, er, um . . .'

'NO! Not unless you count the Bugle Street Flasher.'

I was relieved. I read somewhere that the average age for sex is 17, which only gives me a year and a quarter, well, two years if I do it just before I'm eighteen. But I can't imagine getting that far, somehow. I'll just have to be below average in that, like so many other things, as Ms Farthing is constantly pointing out.

'Anyway, you KNOW I'd have TOLD you,' said Aggy.

'I suppose so, it's just that it seems everyone else is getting up to all sorts of stuff and all I've ever done is a V. Small amount of kissing.'

'Some of us haven't even managed that,' said Aggy, huffily.

Oh dear. I always put my foot in it, somehow.

9 pm. Have werked out that if the average age for sex is seventeen and some people get going at twelve, then quite a lot of people don't do it till they're 22. This makes me feel much better.

9.10 pm. Wonder if I have had proper kiss, really.

9.12 pm. Have gathered various words are muttered throughout this kissing process, but you can't hear most of them (they go 'mmmrgh . . . yearrh . . . uuuuhhhh . . .' Etck.)

In the non-fancying kiss (like the one with Brian) these words include 'Mind out, you've just knocked off my cold sore, speared my gum boil, broken my tooth' Etck.

In the fancying kiss they might be more 'You taste sweeter than fudge' or something.

9.24 pm. The secret is whether you fancy someone. If you don't (like me and Brian) then it all goes wrong and you bash noses and clash teeth and it all feels more like two V. Shortsighted people trying to get through a swing door in opposite directions than a romantic encounter. But if you do fancy each other, then, even nose bashing doesn't seem to matter. It's more, um, like nose waffling.

9.30 pm. Think, that was certainly the kiss I shared with Adam, many moons ago before he realized I was werthless lune. But will I get a chance with Fudge-wig?

82

Midnight. Will go to airport on Saturday to meet Fudgewig's plane. Plane arrives at 3.30. Have decided this will be V. Nice surprise for him.

Yess! Only 39 and a half hours to go.

Fri Jan 29
FILM COURSE
BASIL COUNTDOWN: ONE DAY!!

Basil countdown... One day!

Have told Alfonsa about my plan to get paper-round.

'Vereeeee good Letteeee, you arre not a spoiled bratt expecteeeng ze seeelver spoon of life to jus fall plop! into your lap!'

But we decide it'll be a good idea to get some still photographs of my interviewees as well, as I have no experience AT ALL with a video camera. I am aiming as usual for gritty documentary style and am intending to show how terrible life is for kids today, but how much much worse it could be, if there was a war. See what I mean?

But do I have the courage to interview Josef? Realize it's all harder than I thort.

Midnight. In fifteen and a half hours I will be in the arms of Fudgewig (must remember to address him as Basil, or Baz or poss, yr Highness).

1 am: Basil Basil Basil Basil Fudgewig Basil Basil, Bassseeeel. Bazzeeel, Baz. BB luvs LC troo. Baz 4 Letty.

Amazing wot you can do with a name. You can make it sing, leap like salmon in sunshine Etck. Maybe this would even work with Eric.

Sat Jan 30

Interesting Fact: Gandhi, grate Indian leader and
Peace Warrior who helped kick out the British, was
assassinated today in 1948. Am V. Sad to think of
all grate pacifists like him and Martin Luther King
and John Lennon all being murdered. Hope does not
happen to pacifist film makers . . .

Mother snarling, ripping down the remaining
Christmas decorations. Does anybody except her do
a hands turn lift a finger Etck Etck. And after that
lovely birthday supper, too. Wot more does she
want?

But wot do I care?

I am off to see my troo lurve. And with only the
teeniest Hint of Panick to keep my feet on the
ground.

1.30 pm: Only spent three hours getting ready to
meet Basil. Aimed for casual, 'just-threw-on-wot-
was-by-the-bed-and-dashed-here-so-as-not-to-
miss-you' look. Think I achieved this qu well. Took
tube to airport, usual delays Etck Etck, but got
round to arrivals two hours early so not long till
plane arrives.

1.35 pm. Time is going by with speed of cheetah,
as time sometimes does, when you are thinking of

your belurved. (Actually it often goes by with speed of lame slug.)

1.42 pm. Can you get lame slugs?

1.45 pm. Wish had bought some dosh, not just travel card. Am feeling a bit faint for lack of food and water.

1.47 pm. Cheetah has sadly become slug.

1.49 pm. Wonder if I cld do some busking for a cup of tea?

1.51 pm. Will read *War and Peace*. YES. Time will fly like greyhound.

1.52 pm. Sadly, vast weight in bag is not *War and Peace* but make-up bag full of V. Nachural make up. Oh well, will go to Ladies and plaster kisser with light fluffing of Tanno-mug.

1.58 pm. Perluke. The Ladies costs 20p. It is a disgrace. Will now have to wet self and not look nachural either! Will make sure Only Father votes Ken Livingstone in for Mayor so we can get free loos, fair fares Etck.

2 pm. Put on nachural-luking make-up by going up and down in nice shiny lift. V. Good surface akshully and more flattering than mirror, as nice chromey blur does not show up zits.

2.35 pm. Heh Heh. Scouring floors and returned coin slots in phone boxes has yielded V. Princely sum of 42p. Now, shld I have wee or tea?

Midnight. Home at last. What a day! In case you're interested, I had tea. The plane was three hours late. I stood agog, craning flamingo-like neck to watch the passengers disembark. Last one out was Basil, luking ruffled and all the more ravishing for that, in an arm-and-a-leg-suit (well, it had two arms and two legs, but you get my drift) and shades. He hurtled straight by me, despite my pasting on best smile and opening arms wide.

'Basil!' I shrieked in seductively charismatic voice of terrified fruit bat. He turned, bewildered, looking all around. 'It's me, Letty,' I growled in failed attempt at more sultry mode. He stared straight at me.

I took deep yogic breath and composed bod in siren pose.

He walked on.

Huh?

I galloped after him.

'It's ME. LETTY,' I squawked, leaping into his path and flapping arms in wot I hoped was graceful flamingo-like fashion.

He stopped and stared straight at me, baffled.

I continued to squawk and flap. 'Basil. ME. LETTY! Letty Chubb!' I eloquently repeated.

He took off his shades. I thought a hint of disappointment briefly flitted across his gracious brow, but then he broke into a dazzling smile, displaying several rows of immaculately gleaming snappers.

'Letty. What a . . .' (pause) 'lovely surprise.'

'Didn't you see me?' I was crestfallen. My crest had, definitely, fallen.

'Sorry. These shades are a bit fearsome. Stupid of me.' Then, to my amazement, he swept me into his manly arms and delivered a several million watt kiss. When I came up for air, he looked deep into my eyes and said, sorrowfully, 'I suppose I didn't really believe you'd wait for me. Darling Letty.' (Darling. I feel faint.) 'There must be so many others in your life. If I'd had faith in you, instead of burying myself in my work, I'd have postponed my trip and we could have spent some magical time together.'

'Trip?' I squeaked.

'Sorry, yes, it can't be helped. I've only a few minutes to catch the next shuttle.'

'Yeaarghurghummmmm . . . oh,' I said, or something like that. Funny how the brane stops working at times like this.

'Did you pick up the parcels? Darling?'

'Yes,' I breathed. 'Well, no. They'd gone already.'

Basil whistled sharply through his rows of gleaming snappers. (Oh, no, I've annoyed him.) 'Did you phone Sam?' (It's OK, he's just shrugging.)

'Yesssssssss,' I sighed.

'Could you do me one more teeny favour?' (What would you like? Eat razor blades? Wallow in vat of slugs?) 'If you could just take this, to this address. This one is really urgent. In fact, Vital. But you know, you mustn't breathe a word about it. I won't say MI6, but I think you'll get the picture.' He scribbled something feverishly on the parcel '— And this one, to this address.' He scribbled some more. 'Then I won't have to miss the next plane while I organize a courier. I'll make it up to you when I get back, I promise.'

'Of course,' I groaned, weak with love. Or poss, lack of food, water Etck.

'Must dash. I'll ring you tomorrow, I promise.'

This was too quick. I hadn't waited for three weeks to have no conversation at ALL. And only one kiss. Actually, I had to have another of those.

'Basil.' (What could I say that would get his attention?)

'Mmmm?' He glanced at his watch.

'Aggy's been robbed.'

'Oh NO. Little Aggy? That's terrible. Look, give her this.' He reached into his wallet and pulled out a wad of fifty-pound notes, peeled one off and thrust it into my grateful paw. 'Letty,' he whispered, moving close, his hot breath heating my flamingo-like neck. 'I wish I could do more. I will do more. For Aggy. For her family. For all the destitute and struggling of the world.'

89

I thought this seemed a bit strong, but wasn't thinking V. Clearly cos of volcanic neck sensations. He drew me to him.

We kissed.

'When are you back?' I gasped.

'Sunday week,' he said. 'Let's meet.'

Then he was gone.

Delivered the first parcel to behind a dustbin at 33 Railway Cuttings, Neasden. Couldn't decipher the other address, so pocketed parcel (luckily, not the urgent one) and staggered homewards, faint from hunger, thirst and yearning.

1.00 am. Wonder if might get round to full-blown sex before I am 22 after all?

New werd newsflash: Destitute: means poor. Basil will be gude for my vocabulary.

Sun Jan 31
COOKING, GRANNY CHUBB.

! Interesting fact: Guy Fawkes was hanged drawn and quartered, Jan 31 1606. Maybe werld is slightly better place nowadays after all, or wld you still get big crowds enjoying public hangings if they still existed?

Definitely mooning about . . .

So this is what a kiss can be like.

This is wot they mean.

Waterfalls, thunderbolts, fireworks and all that do not get anywhere near.

Oh, moony woony woony moony
Blue ballooney spuny Juney
Spooney looney mooney woo...

Am so mooney, cld hardly strike match for G. Chubb's stove. Wasted six matches. 'Do you know how much a pack of matches cost?' asked Granny Chubb in a V. Kind voice that struck guilt to my soul. 'Did you know a stamp was only 14p ten years ago?' G. Chubb's pension, needless to say, has not kept pace with inflation . . .

But soon I will be married to Basil, who is rich as well as beautiful and will help the world's poor. And especially his beloved's adored granny. The world is a beautiful place.

Get home to find V. Anxious mother. She sits me down and gives me a cup of coffee. She never makes me coffee. Horrible lurch lurches through stomach. Something bad has happened.

'Letty. Something bad has happened.'

'Tell me the worst. Is it Rover?'

'No. It's . . .'

'Not DAD? Or Benjy?' I cry, in panicky tones, partly to cover up embarrassment of putting my cat first . . .

'No. Hazel's mother's just rung. She's run away from home.'

'No! Not Hazel's mum too. Has she gone off with the postman? Not the same postman?' I had visions of three-in-a-van sex-romps with Hazel's mum, Aggy's mum and a special delivery from Postman Pat.

'Not Hazel's mother, silly. Hazel.'

'Hazel's run off with the postman?!' Unlikely.

'No. Letty. Do listen. Hazel's run away from home.

She left a note. Her mother is frantic. She thought, as Hazel's oldest friend, you might know what's behind it.'

'Mandy!' I say, before I have had time to think.

'You mean her old friend who went to Scotland? What's that got to do with it?'

'No. NO.' (Think like lightning, brain frazzles . . .) 'I was thinking of Mandarin, you know, Aggs's little sister. She was saving money to run away to Australia. And it got stolen.'

'What's that got to do with Hazel?'

'Nothing. Nothing. Running away. Train of thought,' I mumbled.

'Well, have you got any clues as to why Hazel might have gone?'

Oh no, I think. No reason at all. Hazel's being bullied at school, bullied at the bus stop. Her one and only true love is in Scotland. And is a girl. Oh, oh, Hazel. But I don't say a thing. I need time to think. And talk to Aggs.

'Well, do you?'

'No. No. Can I see the note?'

'Hazel's mother is coming straight round with it.'

'Oh. Good.' I burst into tears.

I am still in floods when Mrs Appleby screeches her Porsche to a halt and charges in.

'Letty? What's wrong?' she cries.

93

'Hazel,' I sob.

'Hazel,' she sobs, collapsing.

Hazel's folks are obsessed with the material trappings of success like building conservatories Etck instead of buying you nice clothes or feeding the poor (ahem). El Chubb's advice is: remind them of Edith Bunn down the road who houses six children in a room the size of their kitchen table. If this does not shut them up re spending dosh on mad home improvements, then maybe pictures of Third-Werld huts Etck shld do it. Adults today have no real values, moan, whinge and do not see that we teenagers want more stuff.

In Hazel's case, the stuff she needs is time, Lurve Etck.

But despite orl the bad thingz about Hazel's mum and dad, all I feel at this moment is huge ocean of pity for poor Mrs. Appleby washing over *moi*. It is all I can do not to mention Mandy. But I can't betray Hazel yet, not at least until I have spoken to her.

Hazel's mum shows me her note:

Dear Mum and Dad,
I know this will upset you, but everything has got too much. I have to go away for a bit to sort myself out. Please do not try to find me. I will stay alive and get in touch soon. I have taken £1000 from my post office account, so do not worry I can survive.
Hazel.

94

Oh. She didn't even write 'love'.

'*I will stay alive!*' sobbed Hazel's mum.

'But that's good. She could have said "I will End It All",' I offered cheerily.

Mrs Appleby just wept harder. She is always a brittle, anxious sort of person. But not a crier. It was sad, and weird, like seeing something very strong and hard and ordinary, like a road sign or something, just dissolving.

She just kept repeating phrases from Hazel's letter, over and over: '*I know this will upset you.* OH OH OH. If she only knew.'

I did my best to say the right things without giving anything away. I had to talk to Aggy.

'Look, let me come round and see if I can pick up any clues,' I suggested, thinking Hazel might have left some secret thing for me in our old hiding place.

'But WHY, Letty, WHY? Hazel had – has – everything.'

'She wasn't very happy at school.'

'Not happy? At school? But it's the best school in London. One of the best in the whole country.'

'Um, one of the most ex . . . clusive, yes.' (I stopped myself saying expensive. I felt too sorry for her).

'Letty, I think you're wrong there. It's a wonderful school. Very caring, I'm sure I wish you could go there too, poor dear. It must be hard at Sluggs.'

I was touched. But I felt a strong wave of loyalty to Old Sluggs, battling against the odds as it is.

'We-ell, there's bullying everywhere.'

'Yes. In the street. I know, those awful girls from the estate. But not at St Cheynganggs. I don't think so.' (pause). 'Now, Letty, please be truthful. Is there – a BOY involved?'

'No. No. Definitely not. No boy. I would have known.'

'What a relief.'

(For us both.)

So far the police have been not much more help to Mrs Appleby than to old Aggs's family, partly because of the note. There's millions of teenagers running away, apparently, and they don't make that much of it if there's a sane kind of note and they haven't been abducted.

Have fleeting panick that Hazel *has* been abducted. Is it possible? Her dad is rich enuf to ransom. Perhaps the kidnappers made her write a note to keep the cops Etck off the scent until they have whisked her away to Transylvania or somewhere from where they will send little fingernail clippings and eventually whole fingers to get a ransom. Do not mention this Worry to Mrs Appleby as feel it wld not be good for her sanity. Now, I just can't wait for her to go. Which she soon does, talking of combing the country with Private Detectives . . .

Ring Aggs immediately.

'Well, she's obviously absconded with Mandy,'

sez Aggy, not that bothered.

'But wouldn't she have told us?'

'No. She'd have wanted to make sure it worked. The only way to have a secret is not to tell anyone.'

'But her poor mother.'

'Yeah. It's bad when they go. Really bad . . .'

'But at least you knew why your mother had gone.'

'Yeah. We knew she preferred the postman to us. That made it MUCH better.'

'OK. OK. But we ought to find out. Suppose she has been kidnapped and the note was just a bluff.'

'I'll think about it. Let's go over after school tomorrow.'

So that's what we'll do.

Mon Feb 1
MATHS WORKSHOP

Up at 5.30 to do paper-round. Bike has flat tyre. Arrive 10 mins late. Mr Patel not impressed.

'We have plenty of kids crazy to do this,' he said, beadily. 'If you are late again, the job goes to Elsie.'

I'm not letting vile Elsie have my job.

Tomorrow, grue, is Parents Evening, but this means wilde activity at skule today. Battalions of cleaners, dinner ladies Etck are marched in, at vast expense from funds saved specially for this purpose (nicked from Special Needs). Loos are hosed down with sheep-dip solution to remove graffiti, tampon sculptures are blown up by army disposal units, and loo rolls are introduced for one day only. Those too disgusting are put out of bounds to parentz and guarded by the biggest boyz in skule. A handful of these boyz are even bigger than Dion 'Grotto' Snoggs. I am scared to go within ten metres of them in broad daylight, so they shld keep a few mealy mouthed parents at bay OK.

Portillo gives us V. Big speech about luking perlite and wearing skule uniform right way round Etck. It's a craze at the moment to wear blazers on backwards, but if you've got enormous bazoombers like Aggy it is V. Uncomfy.

Graffiti that won't come off the corridors is covered by 'artwerk'. Portillo is V. Keen to have some cheery luking pix, but Teenage Worriers today are more interested in Damien Hirst, Tracey Emin Etck so the entrance hall is decorated with old mattresses and lots of photos of dead sharks and cows' entrails. Portillo has organized the skule band to play. Yum Yum. They are the Gangsta-Stagbeetles, who are all drummers. At the last minute he chickens out and persuades Mrs Thrombosis to agree to play the piano for some V. Drippy gurlz to sing 'classical melodies'.

After all this we are told that we get to go home early tomorrow as long as we behave nicely for the two hours that poor prospective parents toil round skule. Twenty-five kidz are excluded for the day and given pocket money from Special Needs to stay away from skule.

Impossible to think of anything except Hazel all day. Do think, with small yearn, of Basil, but he hasn't rung. Boyz never do.

Have long talk with Aggs about Hazel. Must say, if Hazel had been whisked off by a lecherous old rat bag after her money, we wld have had no doubts about telling her folks and rescuing her from fate worse than banana, but young romantick forbidden lesbian lurve is a thornier problem. I mean, Hazel is likely to be much happier in arms of Mandy amid the grouse moors than languishing in her foul skule amid posh gurls whose idea of a good time is getting their parents to sack the servants.

Hazel, age 8?. The Applebys love Hazel – but they do not know her... she always HATED ballet!

9.30 pm. Just got back from harrowing visit to Hazel's house with Aggy.

Mr and Mrs Appleby, normally so keen and brisk, are shadows of their former shadows. Her father, hollow-eyed, berates himself about all the times he missed her birthday, skule outings, Etck Etck to go to meetings.

Her mother, voice croaky like aged lizard, starts getting out the photos . . . Hazel at ballet (Hazel always hated ballet), Hazel with hair like white candyfloss in a horrid little peach silk dress with ruffles. Etck. They do love their daughter, but they don't know her, I glumly thort.

Aggs and me finally escape to ransack Hazel's rume for clues. I was sure she wld have left me a note in our secret place, which now, for the first time, I reveal to Aggy. It is a brilliant hide-out that Hazel and I have used since we were tiny. You have to pull up a corner of her carpet and there is a loose board. Under it, there is a huge space in the rafters, big enuf for two people to sit in.

As I pull up the floorboards, I have a horrible lurch. Suppose Hazel got in here and couldn't get out? Or she has been murdered and put in here and will be a skellington? Tremblingly, I raise the floorboards and peer within. Her little Sparkly girly torch I gave her when we were nine is hanging, as usual, from a nail. I flick it on with bated breath, well, with the switch actually.

Phew. No skellington. Realize have been reading

too many krap newspapers lately which has overstimulated my tremulous Teenage Worrier's imagination. But although there is no skellington, there are the following:

A paper bag.

A little box.

About twenty notebooks.

A holdall.

I heave them out while Aggy keeps watch.

I leaf through the notebooks. They are diaries. One is for this year.

'Find anything?' the anguished tones of Mrs Appleby echo along the hall.

Guiltily, I pocket the diary while Aggy places herself firmly behind Hazel's door.

Mrs Appleby rattles the handle.

'Sorry, the door seems to be stuck,' squeaks Aggy, wedging it with her foot as I pocket the box and the paper bag and look quickly through the holdall. Only clothes. I bang the floorboard back while Aggy covers up by having loud coughing fit and rattling door handle in convincing sounding attempt to open it.

As I roll the carpet back, so Aggy steps back and poor Mrs Appleby, as if she hasn't enuf to Worry about, hurtles into rume and falls flat on the shag pile, breaking her hairdo.

We escape back to my place to look through Hazel's stuff.

The paper bag makes me lose it completely. 'It's our sweeties,' I bawl.

'OUR sweeties?' Aggy is baffled.

'Rainbow Bunnies,' I sob, holding up the little multi-coloured sugar rabbits that Hazel and I used to buy every Saturday. Was surprised how well they had lasted. Eight years of preservatives, I s'pose.

But the box is even worse.

It is like a box of my childhood, not just Hazel's. Pix of us on swings, at circus, at every birthday party up till twelve . . . A card I sent her when she had measles . . . Of course, there was other stuff, including all the jolly photos of Mandy, pics of her with me and Aggs, letters from penfrendz Etc. Precious mementos. Hazel . . .

Midnight: I don't know why, but I didn't tell Aggy about the diary. I suppose I thought I'd tell her later. But I don't know if I will. There is stuff in there about Hazel wishing she was at Sluggs with us and hating her home and parents that is just too upsetting. She is completely freaked out by exam pressure. She sounds V. Unhappy, much more than I realized. But at least it confirms she wants to run off with Mandy. Which is a big relief. I'll have to go and find her.

Somehow.

I don't want her to know I ever read this, ever.

Tue Feb 2

Up at 5.15 to do paper-round. Arrive 20 mins early. Mr Patel V. Impressed. Not sure how much longer I can keep this up if long, tortured nights are going to be spent Worrying about Hazel and Baz, Bazel and Haz, maybe this is how Alzheimer's starts . . .

Decide, with Aggs at lunch, that one of us must go to Scotland and rescue Hazel. Since I have just about enuf money for the train fare and Aggy has none, then it will have to be *moi*.

Quickly realize this is easier to declare (woo-hoo!!) than to carry out, due to ignorance of any kind of journey longer than getting to Alfonsa's film course (got lost first time I went to that anyway), fear of Alien World of ticket-collectors, suspicious police, wandering lunies, drunks and enthusiasts for underage sex.

However, it is a V. Imp part of Yuman Nature for the Heart to be able to triumph over the Trembling Hand, and for that matter Leg, Hed, Berm, Knees and most other partz. We are the only ones who can help Hazel, and we owe it to her to try, whether she likes it or not. (Fear this may also be the generous spirit that leads people to cross old ladies over streets they never wanted to cross in the first place, but suppress this Worry.)

She must be in Scotland, I tell Aggy. It's the only possibility. But we can't tell on her. At least, she did write a note. We try to imagine how even more gharstly it wld have been for the old Applebys if she'd just vanished Without Trace.

Decide to bunk off skule, but think better of it. Bound to be reported. Something always goes wrong when you bunk off. You find Portillo's on the train to Scotland or something.

Will go on Saturday.

Have to admit skule is qu fun on Prospective Parents Day, as all the gullible hopeful mums and dads trawl through acres of smiling kleen kidz and quiet perlite teechers and sparkling classrumes with excellent werk all laid out and think this is wot Sluggs is like on a normal day, not realizing the vast effort and bribery that has gone into it.

However, if Portillo was hoping to attract a better class of parent with Mrs Thrombosis and her drippy gurlz he has another think coming – two members of the accompanying wind instruments ensemble were playing their recorders with their noses (this is quite fun and not as hard as it lukes) and someone had tinkered with the piano so it made V. Strange noise like dead aardvark being struck by soyaburger.

Mrs Thrombosis inspected the piano strings and withdrew eighteen erasers. Well, at least class 11F cannot get ye blame for that. All ours have been confiscated.

Still no news of Aggy's robbers, but the police say there have been loads of robberies in Aggy's area . . . Aggy and me decide to keep watch on Fri night, after film course.

Wed Feb 3

Paper-round getting on my nerves. Am too knackered, it's too cold. Think got papers mixed up. Got Benjy to bed V. Early by nasty trick of winding clocks forward to convince him it was way past his bedtime. He seems to read clocks V. Well for his age so can't be dyslexic, surely, despite Only Mother's constant Fears.

Hazel Worry continues. Becomes so intense that almost forget to pick phone up when it rings. And when hearing Hazel's voice (for it is she) do double-take to start with, wondering if it is dream voice inside Hed. Eventually manage to squawk:

'Hazel! Where ARE you?'

'Can't say.'

'Hazel, I'm your BF. Wot do you mean you can't say?!'

'Oh. Thought that was Aggy.'

'You both are. You know that.' (It's not my fault we got broken up when Hazel went off to poncey old St Cheynganggs.)

'We're going to run away together.'

'What are you talking about? You have run away. You mean you and Mandy?'

Silence.

'Look. If you tell my parents I'll KILL you.'

108

'Haze, I must. They're going bananas.'

'Whose happiness is more important, theirs or mine?'

'Well. Are you all right?'

'I'm fine. But I need some stuff. I didn't get organized.'

'Look, come back, Hazel. I'll tell your folks. They'll be so pleased you're alive they'll probably invite Mandy to come and live with you. Times have changed, Hazel.'

'You don't know my mum and dad.'

'I've known them since I was four.'

'Look, Letty, I haven't told you everything. It's too complicated. Please just help.'

I am torn.

'Go round to my house and you can get my stuff. It's just an old holdall full of clothes that I left in our old hiding place. Say you just want to see if there are any clues, you know, like I might have left a note for you or something.'

'Oh. Haze, I feel bad about it. I've already DONE that. What do you think? I'd just hang around waiting for you to come back? Your mum's going up the wall.'

'You got my stuff already?' There's a note of Panick. 'You didn't read my DIARIES!!!?'

'Course not,' I mutter, crossing my fingers and blushing. I am a bad liar, but luckily she can't see me. 'I went to find clues, Haze, whaddya think I'd do? Just sit round waiting for your kidnapper to send

109

the ransom note? And your mum is going completely mental.'

Silence.

'Is she?'

'She's beside herself, Hazel. So's your dad.'

'OK. Look. You can tell them I phoned if you like. Say I'm fine. Say I'll be in touch soon.'

'Hazel, are you in Scotland?'

Silence.

That means she is. And that means Edinburgh. And I know which school Mandy's at. Must think.

'Look, Hazel, you're mad. If I don't know where you are, how can I send you the stuff?'

'You can send it to a PO Box. I'll give you the number.'

Now, at last, for once, I am decisive. 'I'm coming up to Scotland on Saturday. I'll be at Edinburgh station between . . .' I think, wildly, it must be about five hours journey . . . 'between 1 and 2. If you're not there, I'll be all alone and lost and miserable and sold into slavery probably. If you CARE, you'll meet me. OK. I WON'T tell anyone. I WON'T bring anyone. Just BE there OK?'

'There's no point, Letty. I'm not coming home.'

'Exactly. If you won't come and see me, I'll have to come and see you.'

'But, Letty, it's nuts. All I need is my stuff, I'm perfectly FINE.'

But there is a tremor in her voice.

'Of course you are, Hazel, but I'm coming anyway.

110

OK?'

'Well, I suppose I can't stop you.'

'See you Saturday.'

'Maybe.'

'You'd better not leave me shivering on the station.'

'Oh, Mandy! Mandy's here!' Hazel's voice went up about two zillion octaves into an ecstatic whoop and whistled off into the stratosphere. (**NB new werd**, meaning the layer of air above the earth's atmosphere.) 'Byeeeeeee!'

'Bye, for now then, Haze. Be there.'

But she'd already put the phone down. I dialled 1471. But of course 'the caller withheld their number'.

Well, at least she sounds OK. And I know she will come to the station. I think.

I go to bed V. Shaky.

Cannot sleep.

Thur Feb 4

Oh, bottoms.

Was up at 5.30. Arrived dead on time. Elsie there, smirking. Mr Patel volcanic. Apparently he had a call from Mrs Bunn saying she had a dirty magazine delivered yesterday.

'But I don't deliver dirty mags.'

'No. Not any more,' sez Mr Patel firmly.

Elsie smirks more. Perluke. Obviously she sneaked round with a copy of *Wet Shellsuits*, or whatever, and stuffed it through poor old Mrs Bunn's letter box so she cld steal my paper-round.

It is a cut-throat world.

Well, I won't have to do my krap paper-round on Sat then and can leave for Scotland at crack of dawn.

Fri Feb 5
FILM COURSE

An airmail letter from my Chinese penfriend:

> Hello Letty,
> My English much gooder than your Chinese, no? My English spelling better also as well, I think. Ha ha. I hope you and your Basil (such a beautiful name) have a blissful sexing and that he is a good smart boy that your mother also likes.
>
> I doing well at school. I do very well: arithmetic, physics, astronomy, dancing, painting, agricultural studies. What is your doing best at?

I like very much your photo and your big nose and lovely spider legs. Your hair is funny too and my boyfriend laughs a lot when he see you and say are all English girls have frog eyes?

He is so funny and kind.

I hope very soon to visit you in your big home with my family.

Your best friend.

Lotus

I think I will tell her we are moving to Australia.

Alfonsa has dedicated most of the course this week to practical werk so after a brief and dazzling lektcher, she sez I can do interviews. I am starting with Stanley. Will do Saul Spangle, aftcr, then next week, Kurt Flasher and Bageshott Hardy. Intercut that lot with Syd Snoggs and some posh boyz and Bob's your uncle.

Of course, I know I must interview Josef too. It's just that it will be so hard . . .

Have decided, since Stanley is such a round quiet person, that I will only use stills of him anyway, as he is too shy to respond well in front of camera. So just decide to tape him for the moment. Even so, he asks if we can go somewhere V. Quiet and private. How sweet. I suggest the park. But he sez his house wld be better as no-one can eavesdrop and it's only round the corner from the film course. Decide, good idea, as if Ruth'n'Van'n'Elsie came upon me tape recording Stanley in the park, my life would cease to be werth living.

Stanley's house V. Nice, lots of stripped pine, spotlights, kool photos everywhere. Obv V. Arty family.

'Let's go to my room in case my parents come home,' he sez.

His rume is V.V. Kool. Mainly computer stuff and more kool photos. He sits very shyly on a cushion on the floor and I turn on the tape.

'So. You have been called up to fight, Stanley. How do you feel?' I begin.

'Horny,' he squeaks. And lunges at me.

Before I know what is happening, he has got his hand right up my jumper. For a second I am too surprised to do anything and that second is too long, cos as his first hand failed to find anything under my jumper he has now got his other hand somewhere else. I scream at him and push him away, really furious.

'Sorry. Sorry. Sorry,' he whimpers. 'Sorry sorry sorry. Thought you wanted to, sorry.'

I stomp downstairs in a rage and storm off.

Pluke Pluke triple Pluke. I left the tape recorder.

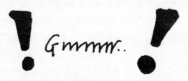

The record of my great interviews with boyz so far:

'So. You have been called up to fight, Stanley. How do you feel?'

'Horny.'

Great.

10.30 pm. Stand freezing on corner of Aggs's street to see if we can spot likely burglars. A group of blokes wearing masks approach, carrying big sacks with 'swag' and 'loot' written on them. For a moment we can't believe our luck.

'Ullo mate,' sez the biggest. 'D'you know where Mimosa Crescent is?'

We are frozen to spot, hearts pounding like, um, hearts. Panick surges within my feeble frame.

A bishop comes round the corner. 'Oh, follow me,' he says, giving a little skip.

Of course, they are off to a fancy-dress do.

We stand there another hour. All we have is a packet of stale Cheesy Wotnots.

'Letty, you should go home. Scotland tomorrow.'

Aggs is the best.

Sat Feb 6

Right. Operation Braveheart.

SCOTLAND, wahey!

Have told Only Mother I am going off at crack of dawn on a film thingy and then spending Saturday night with Aggs. If I call her in the evening, I might be able to head her off from ringing Aggs' house to find out if I've cleaned my teeth or something. This alibi's full of holes, but I do stay with Aggs occasionally and Only Mother trusts her as a brainiac who doesn't spend her evenings behind the bicycle sheds with rampant Boyz or drug-dealers, so it just might werk. Perhaps in such a Noble Cause as this, the gods and goddesses will be on our side, though they usually aren't, werse luck.

V. Glumey that Aggs can't come too but my spindly savings will hardly run to this and there's no way she can afford it.

Get up at 4.00 am. Fall over Benjy, who is going for a wee in total darkness, risky business. Shut him up with promise of ten packs of Sherbert Burps on my return. Fall over Rover, who is invisible but sounds V. Aggrieved. Shut same up with promises of Fatto Catto, which seems to do the trick. Tiptoe past Only Parents' rume, deafened by symphony of snoring, groning, muttered recriminations at injustices of werld Etck (hoping middle age of *moi* is better than this). So much for them springing up to see their gallant offspring set off into crazy werld of film-making Etck. (Have almost convinced Self of alibi). Check pathetick money supply, apple for journey, brane for journey Etck. All seems to be as much in order as it will ever be.

Walk to tube. Amazed that first tubes in morning, instead of being full of snoring drunks, shouting lunies, dead bodies Etck, are busy with V. Dutiful-looking, grey-complexioned folk reading newspapers and obv going to the kind of jobs that you or I might prefer to do without on a regular basis.

By 6.00 at King's X, ie: while Adored Parents still snore and grone, the Reel Werld is humming with life. Decide to really slum it, on the grounds that nobody I care about can see me. Buy armfuls of *Smirk*,

Weenybop Etck with remains of savings.

Get on train stumbling under weight of same. Experience thrill of independence as train pulls out through grubby suburbs and subby gruburbs and gathers speed though leafy greenbelt (griefy leanbelt, this is qu fun) uninhabited except for hypermarket carparks. Feel weird stuff you feel when you luke into so many back yards and gardens and windows and realize they are all filled with people carrying vast bags of hopes dreamz and wishes just like you. Feel V. Small and V. Big at same time – part of vast world, yet smaller than ant's paw. (Do ants have paws? Or feet?)

Wish I was going up to wonderful Hogwarts school with loads of nice wizards, potions, magick, scary times but good frendz, happy endings, all that. Or, even better, going to Arctic North to mingle with armoured bears Etck. But this, sadly, is just reel life.

Urban wastescape thins out to reveal noble sweeps of nachure. Gaze out of window at happy little sheep,

placid little cows Etck. Just mooing and noshing all day with no Worries. Realize there must be more ants than people in werld. Prob more ants in single field. In fact, realize have read somewhere that if you put all ants in werld on one side of scales and weighed them against all people in werld the ants wld weigh more. Wonder if ants experience cosmic glume?

Feelings of loneliness quickly dispelled by lively background noise of train journey, mobile phones ringing, computers bleeping, people arguing about reserved seats, football fans ripping open first beercans of the day Etck. Struck by stupidity of people going on about what a little country England is, lukes vast to *moi*, rolling countryside, towns I've never heard of with awesome cathedrals rearing up out of them, big rivers crossed by giant bridges Etck. Hardly luke at *Smirk*, *Weenybop* Etck, except V. Concentratedly when sat next to by wheezing young man size of hippo, whose hed I sense constantly turning hopefully to *moi* without being able to see it, you know the way you do.

Decide only way to avoid luming conversation with hippo-boy is to feign (**NB New Werd**, meaning 'pretend') sleep.

Wake in Panick. So much for feigning then. How many hours have passed? Train is zooming through lonesome landscape. Obviously, have missed Edinburgh and am hurtling through Highlands to Isle of Skye Etck and no bonny boat, bonny Prince Charlie or nuffink . . . But hooray, soothing announcement:

'The next station is Steppington Bumbleby. We should reach Steppington Bumbleby in ten minutes.'

'Er, what'd he say?' I ask hippo-boy, only to see that hippo boy has been replaced by giraffe woman – a creature of such awesome neck length that even flamingo-necked *moi* has to shout my question twice more before she can hear me. Luckily her extra height has helped her to decipher train announcement, bringing her ears closer to the speakers than those of ordinary mortals.

Hippo-boy has been replaced by Giraffe-woman...

'We're just coming into Waverley, hen,' she smiles.

Phew.

Scottish people use 'hen', I have discovered, like we use 'duck'.

Get off train, clutching Hazel's holdall and bag with my own pathetick travel kit. Shiver on the platform for ages until everybody else has gone. Nothing happens. Starving and thirsty. Check remains of miniscule Operation Braveheart fund, decide there's enuf to get a sandwich in the caff, and can still keep an eye on the platform for Hazel. Wonder what I'll do if she doesn't come. Wonder what will happen to our friendship now. Wonder a lot of things.

After what seems like hours, realize a boy of about twelve, ceaselessly picking his hooter, has been hovering about outside, luking in at *moi*. Luke at him. Lukes at *moi* as if I had crawled out from under stone, but eventually comes in.

'Hazel,' he sez, V. Firmly.

'Letty,' I say, as firmly as poss back. He lukes contemptuous. Points in vague direction out of station with contemptuous finger.

'Hazel,' he sez again.

Feel V. Supicious and nervous, but also feel sure he must be some messenger from Hazel. He beckons again, and I follow him.

I'm in a strange town with no money and no sense, and the only connection I have is with a weird boy who might know where Hazel is.

After trudging up and down endless hills and winding streets, the boy stops me on a corner and points up to a grimy window.

The curtain moves to reveal Hazel, beckoning.

Am now certain I am in the grippe of some horrible kidnapping plot and that Hazel is being held from behind with gun to head.

I do not move.

Eventually, Hazel throws open the window.

'Are you mad, Letty? It's freezing! Come on up!'

Oh well. Perhaps better to have gun to hed in warmth than die of hypothermia. I approach creepy little door which is ajar. The letter lying on the doormat I wouldn't normally have even noticed, except for the name written on it, which leapt up at me like when you stand on the wrong end of a garden rake.

B. Barrington. ArghhhhH!

Whaaaaaaaaaaaaaaaaaaaat?

Hyperventilating I go up creepy little stairs.

Hazel flings herself upon me.

'Sorry, Letty. I had to make sure you were alone.'

'Would I lie to you?'

'Sorry. Sorry. Here.' And she shoves a big bag of fudge (ooh, clotted cream vanilla) at me.

But fudge is not going to quell my suspicions. I

launch straight in like rattlesnake.

'Hazel, have you seen Basil since you've been here?'

'Basil? No, of course not.'

'Are you sure?'

'Of course. Why are you asking me this? Did you just come all the way up here to tell me how paranoid you are about boyz?'

'Then why is there a letter addressed to him on the doormat?'

Silence. Then: 'Can't we talk about something else?'

This was a horrible moment for *moi*. I've known Hazel since nursery. She can no more lie to me than fly. Her eyes were skidding round the room (well, you know what I mean, they were NOT meeting mine) and her cheeks were a nasty puce. I couldn't leave it alone.

'Hazel! I didn't come all the way to Scotland to be lied to! What do you think I am?' I could feel my eyes stinging with tears. Tears of bewilderment and betrayal.

Hazel froze.

I felt nauseous. Twelve years of friendship were spinning away, out of my control. I gave it one more go. I grabbed her wrist. 'You've got to tell me! You've GOT to!'

'Oh all right! All right! This flat is Basil's! Yes! He put me up here!'

'How could you? How could you?'

'But it's not what you think! Letty I promise! I

only didn't want you to know because I thought you'd be hurt . . .'

'Too right!' I stormed. Hurt? I was breaking up in places I didn't know I had.

'Letty. You must listen. I've got nothing going with Basil. It's just I bumped into him after the New Year's Eve party and we got talking and he mentioned he had a flat here and I asked if I could use it for a bit. That's how I knew I could run away! I'd never have dared to, otherwise.'

'Oh, sure. And what did he want in return?'

'Nothing. Nothing!' Then Hazel collapsed in tears.

'All right, cry, I thought you reckoned gurlz ought to be above all that.'

'MANDY'S DUMPED ME!' Hazel exploded through her tears. 'I don't want to stay in bloody Edinburgh. I was lonely in this flat even when it was possible to see Mandy every now and again, but now it's . . . it's . . .' (more tears)

'Mandy has dumped you?'

'She's fallen in love with an older woman of eighteen.'

'Unbeleeevable. I didn't know lesbians were so cruel.'

'They're no crueller than anyone else,' snapped Hazel furiously.

'No. Then why not come home?'

But she cannot face returning. Now it was clear to me why she sounded so excited at Mandy coming in when she rang me in London. Mandy had told her they had to talk, that things weren't quite the same. Hazel had been desperate. Then, when Mandy had shown up, she'd thought everything was going to be OK. But no. Oh, pooor Hazel. She feels a failure, nothing will ever be OK again. She can't tell her parents the truth, she doesn't want to lie, she is bereft.

'Well, I'm not going to leave you, Hazel.'

'But I can't go home.'

Realized at this moment what that cosy word 'home' akshully means to Hazel. Exams, pressure, hiding her sexuality. Not so cosy after all.

'But where will you stay?'

'Here.'

'Here?'

We luked round the rume. It was about six foot wide by seven foot long. The walls were a pale greyish yellow, crisscrossed with a thousand cracks and encrusted with damp fungussy green eruptions. The curtain hung in tatters about the grimy rotting window frame. Water dripped through the ceiling into a variety of old pans and chipped saucers. An icy gale blew through the cracked window. The little iron bedstead was covered in a flimsy rag, that appeared to have spent its earlier life as a dishcloth. It smelt, like all such rumes, of boiled cabbage and wee.

Felt V. Strange about this dump belonging to Basil. Didn't feel like the person I know and lurve at all. But Hazel's situation was more Imp. Just at this moment.

I believed her about Basil, I don't know why considering how byootiful she is, but I've known her long enough to know how honest she is too.

'Hazel. You've got one thousand pounds. Why are you staying here? You'd be better off on the streets.'

'Do you know how much rents are? This place is *free*! A thousand pounds could last me nearly a year if I stay here . . .'

'And don't eat.' I luked at her. I realized how thin and pale my shiny Hazel had become. 'Are you eating?'

'I can't eat. I haven't eaten for two days.'

I took charge. I became like those people you read about and wish you were, but never are. Firmly but Fairly I packed Hazel's belongings into an old carrier bag. It was sad. A photo of Mandy, a comb, a toothbrush, a pair of pants. Firmly but Fairly, I marched her to the station cafe, sat her in front of a bowl of nourishing croissant, spoon fed it to her.

Firmly but Fairly I reassured her that I wouldn't tell her parents what had happened – yet. Firmly but Fairly I said we would find somewhere for her in London. Inside, however, I was shaking like a leaf. Hazel had always been so beautiful, so together, so gorgeous in every way . . .

We catch a train to London – it'll get us in early enough in the evening for us to try to find Hazel a room for the night.

On the way down, the conversation not surprisingly turns to Basil.

'But he's got this flash job hasn't he? Why's his place such a tip?'

'It's just a little pied-a-terre. He's going to do it up. He's got big plans. He's very clever, isn't he?' purrs Hazel, warmed by friendship and her croissant. I am warmed, too. He *is* very clever, and alarmingly charming.

'Hazel . . . Promise. Promise you didn't, you know, see anyone else with Baz, you know, like a girlfriend? NOTHING like that at all?'

'Letty, I promise.'

Pher-ew.

When we get to London I bundle Hazel onto the bus. I have decided where to go: Aggy's. As usual, the lifts are broken. We drag ourselves up the manky old staircase, clambering over drunks and people injecting themselves. Aggy has to do this every day. And her little brothers and sisters.

I hide Hazel in the corridor and ring Aggy's bell. Fortunately it's her that opens the door.

'Shhhhh.'

We tiptoe in. Aggy puts down the hammer. She doesn't open the door without it since the burglary.

'Haze. You look terrible.'

Hazel collapses, weeping. Akshully, she doesn't look bad now, she still looks like a heroine of those old movies – soft tears tenderly decorating softer cheeks Etck. But then she always does. Ponder wot use it is luking like Hazel when your only heart is breaking. Better to be ugly and happy, like El Chubb. If I was happy, that is . . .

'I can't go home,' says Hazel, between sobs. 'I can't face them.'

'You can stay here,' sez Aggy, 'while we work something out.'

'Oh, Aggy. But you've no room.'

'There's room in my heeeeart,' carols Aggy.

Hazel lets a ghost-of-a-smile suffuse her quivering mug.

'But what will your dad say?' I Worry.

'Yeah,' ponders Aggy. 'He won't harbour a runaway. Well, I'll have to hide you.' Hide? Aggs shares her bedrume with four little kids. 'There's a loft above the top flat,' sez Aggs. 'People store old mattresses and stuff up there. We could make you a cosy nest. Just while you get yourself together. Then me and Letty will take you home and stand by you while you tell your folks everything.' Aggy pauses as she catches Hazel's anguished look and adds, 'Or make up some story.'

'Oh, Aggs. Oh, thanks,' is all Hazel can manage.

We sneak upstairs and make a little nest among the old mattresses. I am reminded of the skule entrance on new parents day. But it is a lot cosier for Hazel than being on her own in Edinburgh, living in Basil's horrible flat. Grue, fret Etck. When the dust clears from all this, Sherlock Chubb has some investigating to do.

We feel about ten again, building the little den.

'What if people come up looking for their old stuff?' sez Hazel.

'Just say you're doing the same. Anyway, most of this stuff's been up here for years.'

'Aggy, I don't know how to thank you.'

'Thanks will do fine,' blushes Aggs.

'Hazel, I've got to find out more about Basil. Like, why didn't he arrange to meet me? In Scotland?'

But there was no reply. Hazel had fallen into a deep sleep.

Rang Only Mother to say I was back safe at Aggy's.

Aggy found me an old coat to sleep on. Unfortunately there wasn't a spare coat to put on top. V. Cold.

Midnight. I do believe Hazel doesn't have thing with Basil. I think.

Or do I?

12.10. Yes, I do. She lied at first, then she didn't. Anyway, it's crazy of me to think she would start fancying boyz again. She hasn't, for ages, if she ever really did.

12.35. Well. If Basil doesn't come round tomorrow, I'll know he doesn't care. And if he does, I'll ask him. That's the best Sherlock Chubb Marple can manage. Will now fall into welcoming arms of slumber. Am too tired to . . .

Sun Feb 7
COOKING, GRANNY CHUBB

Interesting Fact: Birth of Charles Dickens, author of grate musical Oliver! Etck, arf arf. He was born in 1812, when they still had loads of public hangings. He had twelve children and almost as many books.

Forgot to tell Granny Chubb I wasn't coming. She'd bought some sprouts specially, to show me how to top and tail them. So I didn't miss much.

Snuck back home at crack of dawn. Limbs like lead. I don't know how Aggy sleeps a wink with all those kids in her rume, falling out of bed, going for wees, losing their teddies Etck. How lucky I am only to have Benjy and Rover waking me up.

Basil is calling to collect me tonight, if he remembered the date he made that strange day at the airport. Am Quaking like leaf. In fact, am like walking zombie all day as Mother so tactfully points out.

'You look like a walking zombie,' she says. 'I think you'd better cancel your date.'

No way. Spend three hours in bath, anointing self with unguents Etck, then do usual old hoovering and polishing of wig, mug Etck and end up luking slightly werse than before. Oh, I'm too tired to be that bothered. Really.

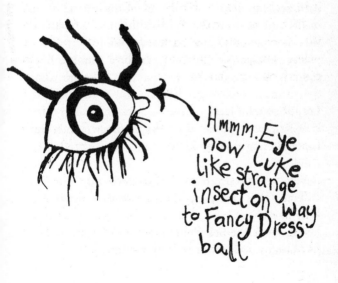

Hmmm. Eye now Luke like strange insect on way to Fancy Dress ball

7.30 pm. Baz calls to collect me, looking like 1930s crooner in fab dark suit. Mother all wimpy and blushing as she ushers him in. Have spent ages scrubbing kitchen floor and covering pale blue chipped formica table with nearly clean sheet. Stuffed jug of flowers on top. In candlelight our kitchen looks almost bourgeois. Have never felt ashamed of hovel before, but werldly thoughts of this sort seem less important right now than my mixed feelings about the mysterious Baz. But, phew . . . he's so rich, smart, sofistercated and Etck. Except for that place in Edinburgh of course. But then he's a busy man, and he seems to have no Other Half (pheww, sigh Etck) to help him take care of the boring details of life like that. When He Is Mine, I will be able to lift some of the weight off his shoulders . . .

Slight romantick anti-climax for a minute, for as soon as we are out of the door, he asks me about delivering the packages he gave me at the airport. I say I'll explain later.

When we get to the restaurant I launch into heartfelt angwish about Hazel, which is all I can think about.

Basil seems irritated but then perks up.

'Hazel. Isn't she the girl I saw you with at the New Year party?'

'Yes. Isn't she beautiful?'

'Didn't notice. And is she very unhappy?'

'Very.' There is a long silence. 'And she's in your flat.'

Basil squeezes my hand and about five thousand fireworks go off in a little spot just under my neck. Wonder if I have discovered a new erogenous zone?

'Oh, of course, that Hazel.'

'Yes. That Hazel.'

'Oh Letty!' (squeeze, squeeze) 'You're not jealous of Hazel!'

'Jealous? Of course not. I just wondered why you put her up in your flat.'

'Oh. That.' (squeeze, squeeze)

'Mmmm. That.' (Squirm squirm) By now, I could hardly breathe, what with the squeezing and the melting hot breath and my mingled emotions Etck.

But Basil launched into an elegant eloquent account of how he bumped into Hazel after the party and recognized her as my friend. 'I thought, you see, that if I was kind to her, she'd tell you and it would give me a chance to get to know you better. And,' he blushed modestly, 'that it would make you think well of me. Also, I really wanted to help her. It is not only the poor who have troubles in this wicked world, Letty, the rich also have hearts that can be broken, and souls in anguish. And Hazel really is a poor little rich girl.'

How troo, how troo. Basil is so warm and kind. How could *moi* have thought badly of him, even for an instant? Still, must confirm that the instant had a way of lengthening itself into a few moments more . . .

'And did you really not find Hazel beautiful?'

'Oh. A bit too Barbie doll for me. I am an eesthete, certainly; but I like character in a face – and wisdom. And intelligence as well as beauty, like you.'

My hed swam in ocean of lurve. (But wot is an *eesthete*?)

Basil was telling me about his recent trip to Azerbaijan to fix up a website. He is V. Clever and technical, also V. Keen on helping peasants Etck to communicate across cyberspace and find Freedom. Was just beginning to see him as Saviour of werld, but a mixture of knee squeezing, red wine and exhaustion meant I lost the plot a bit. Anyway, after long political speech about exploitation of masses Etck, he asked for the bill and his remaining airport package.

'You have still got it?'

'Oh. Yeah.'

'Where?'

'In my room.'

'Well, I need it.'

We seemed to be out of the restaurant rather quickly, I must admit. I was hoping for maybe a shoeful of champagne or something, followed by a romantic walk back through the park, starlight in wig, and lots of nuzzling. But Basil seemed a bit preoccupied and brought me straight home.

I thought I'd blown it, but he looked very tenderly at me.

'Darling Letty, I wish I could see more of you,' he said with a luke suggestive of things not mentionable in a family buke such as this. 'And, when this project is over, I will. We'll have long candlelit suppers and romantic starlit walks.' (He's a mindreader! Our minds are beating as one! We have twin souls!) 'Could you just nip up and get my parcel?' he asked gently.

I nipped up.

I couldn't find the parcel.

This was because my rume basically resembles a pile of old socks, which is not surprising cos that is mostly what it is. If you want to find anything you have to burrow into it like a badger, esp if you want to find a pair of socks, which you wld think wld be easy but is akshully the hardest thing to find of all. I feel my rume is an accurate summation of my life to date, a symbol for the state of the inside of my head, which is both a pile of old socks and a pile of old sex, or it would be if the latter had akshully been around for long enough to have got old, moan whinge Etck. I think all this comes down to having been brought up in a family that never tidies up, never buys anything and is beset by Worry and Phobia. Still, we can but dream . . .

I nipped down.

'I can't find it.'

'I'll look. I really need it.'

Kwickly weighed in balance two things: grate excitement of Basil being in my rume and thort of

Pile of socks

My rume

possible ensuing thrills against horror of him seeing how I akshully live. Latter wins.

'You can't. We'll wake Benjy. He often sleeps in there,' I add.

'Ah, Letty, you're too good, and too young, for me,' and he kissed me on the head!

My look of anguish obv got to him though, because he added in V. Sultry voice, 'But soon you won't be.' And nuzzled my neck before proceeding with a very long kiss. 'I'll come round for it first thing, then,' he winked. And was gone.

New werd newsflash: Asked dad what an eesthete was. Word is in fact '**aesthete**' (ahem). Which means 'Professed admirer of the beautiful.' So that's all right then.

3 am. Spent five hours tidying rume.

Even put a couple of dandelions from yard in cup by bed.

Rume has never luked so gude.

Found Basil's package in Horace's cage.

How did it get there?

Luckily, Horace has not shredded it.

Mon Feb 8

7.30 am. Can't believe it, Basil turned up five mins ago.

My mother, staggering about blearily attempting to aim Galaktik Snaks into Benjy's breakfast bowl, reeled as she opened the door. Obv too vain to be seen in muesli-stained old dressing-gown, no make-up Etck, by fudge-wigged siren.

I could hear Belurved's chocolate tones wafting along the hall. 'So sorry to bother you at this unearthly hour, Mrs Chubb, unspeakably rude. Do forgive me. But I left a rather important parcel here and I have an urgent meeting. Oh, what a gorgeous dressing-gown! Where did you get it?'

'Letty!' squeaked my mother. 'It's, er . . .'

'Basil. Basil Barrington.'

I got the package.

'Thank you SO much, Mrs Chubb. Awfully sorry,' Basil charmingly bellowed over my head.

'When will I see you again?' I bravely stuttered.

'Oh, soon, soon. I'll ring you very soon.'

And he was off, into the drizzly dawn . . .

Went round with fude parcel for Hazel after skule. Have kept half of my lunch for her and Aggy has done same. We also got her some crisps and coke.

'Oh, lovely,' she said, gazing at the congealed pizza.

But she is definitely perking up. We try to

138

persuade her it's time to go home. Her parents have stuck notices on all the trees for miles and the longer she leaves it the harder it will be.

'Oh, that's nice,' sez Hazel. 'Like a lost cat.'

Tue Feb 9

Interesting Fact: Conscription began in Britain in 1916. This was when everyone (well, all the blokes, akshully) had to join the army to fight in World War 1, or else they'd be given white feathers Etck to show what cowards they were. Think maybe shld werk this into my film . . .

Wake up to cheery sounds of parents rowing about money, as usual.

'Why don't you get an accountant and save tax?!' shouts my mother.

My Only Father says, who needs accountants, he can work out he's broke perfectly well on his own, just by trying to use his cash card and watching the little screen tell him to go boil his head, but in polite banker language. My Adored Mother responds that having an accountant might shame him into earning enough to pay tax, or at least enough to pay the accountant, and it might be an incentive. In fact, she now wishes he had had the sense to BE an accountant instead of a penniless hack, though I have to say that my Beloved Father would have to be a V. Different, not to say Unrecognizable Person to be a good accountant, since the checkout at Tesco's is usually too much for him.

Take four spring rolls and some salad round to Hazel. Plus two tubes of mintoes.

'Yummy,' she sez. 'Have I got on the radio yet?'

Am beginning to think she is enjoying this.

Aggy gets tough.

'Look at this, Hazel!' She thrusts the local paper in front of Hazel's diminutive and perfectly formed hooter.

ANGUISH OF LOCAL MUM.

Beautiful blonde teenager Hazel Appleby disappeared from her home on blah blah leaving only a note blah blah.

'Where did we go wrong?' wept her mother yesterday. 'She has always been the perfect daughter.' Blah blah blah . . .

Hazel luked at this for some time. Then I saw tear form in the corner of one of her luminous azure peepers. 'Did my mum really say that?' she asked.

Wed Feb 10

BABYSIT

Terrible day at skule. My mock GCSE results are krap.

Ruth, Van'n'Elsie's are even krapper but of course they don't care.

Aggs got ten A stars. She's already done maths and Spanish for real (A stars, of course). So she'll have twelve A stars. Why does a genius want to be my frend?

'It's only cos you moon about and don't work,' she sez.

Thanks. Even my best frend sounds like a teacher now.

As I read *Dr Glume and the Temple of Eville* to Benjy for the forty-fifth time, I ponder the reckidge of my Life to Date.

Have to make a plan. Have decided: will concentrate on making my film V. Gude and the best ever made Etck. Then I will have a bolt hole if I fail all my GCSEs. Will, however, spend every minute of Easter hols revising for GCSEs. Then I am bound to pass enuf to get into film skule.

Ring Aggy about Exam plan.

She sez, she was talking about it to Hazel and Hazel went very quiet and started bawling. Turns out, the main reason she ran away was exam terror. She was doing her mocks this week! So she's missed them!

141

She has been petrified of failing.

So that's what it's all about.

Oooh. Poor Hazel. Imagine being at a skule where nearly everyone gets marks like Aggy. It wld make you feel lower than the lowliest worm. Good side is, since we can't get Hazel to tell her folks about Mandy, we can give her the courage to talk about this. We are going to take her home tomorrow. It's free study period all day, so can do it in morning. Hazel is going to ring her mum tonite. Phew. Couldn't stand the weight of the Applebys' misery much longer. Or the lies.

Thur Feb 11

8 am. Am going to get down to interviewing V. Seriously today. There is a whole afternoon 'Free study' period. Heh Heh. Have a list of eight boyz. But first, off to get Hazel.

4 pm. Phew. Wot a day.

Aggy and me escorted Hazel home at eight thirty. Her mum and dad were standing at the open door, openly weeping. Felt big lump arrive in own throat, as though had just swallowed piece of fudge, whole.

Hazel paused, then ran sobbing into their open arms.

What with me and Aggs, snuffling on the gravel drive, there was a whole lot of crying going on. They won't need to water the garden for weeks.

Was dreading Hazel's dad looking at his watch, picking up his briefcase Etck, but no. The Applebys had both taken the day off work.

Aggy and me stood about not knowing where to look.

Then Hazel turned to us and said: 'I can handle it.'

'But darling,' screeched Mrs Appleby, 'we have to talk to Scarlett and, er, Agatha . . . They know what you've been doing and . . .'

'So do I, Mum,' said Hazel, firmly.

Mrs Appleby likes Hazel to call her 'Mummy'. I don't know why. But she didn't wince, which was a good sign. Mr Appleby put a restraining arm around his wife, and she gulped.

'Thanks girls,' he said to us. 'Thanks very much. We'll all talk soon. I think we need to be alone just now,' he added meaningfully to Mrs A.

Hazel nearly collapsed with relief. You could see all the tension falling off her. Now she had a chance to tell just what she felt she could tell . . .

So me and Aggy sloped off.

Bit of an anti-climax really.

But at least it left plenty of time for interviews with boyz at skule. Aggy agreed to be my minder, to make sure another Stanley incident does not occur. Though must say I can't really imagine any of the Sluggs boyz making a lunge at *moi* in front of the dinner ladies Etck.

Akshully, got some amazing stuff. One boy wrote this, as he didn't want to speak:

I wonder and wonder,
what is a Man?
What is a poor man for?
To date? To mate?
Or to stand and wait
until he is called to war.

I wonder and wonder,
what is a boy?
What is a poor boy for?
To wander, to blunder
In search of joy
Until he is called to war.

I am V. Moooved. Will try to perswade him to read
it out, or maybe cld get Dad to do it and then have
it read as soundtrack to V. Mooving pix of happy
little boyz in football field and dying big boyz in
battlefield.

Another boy goes on about Fear. Sez he wakes in
night sometimes, imagining what it wld be like if he
had to fight.

Another boy goes on a bit more about fear. He is a
Kosovan refugee. He wakes every night. I realize I
will *have* to interview Josef.

Another boy goes on about Strength. It seems boyz
Worry about biceps almost as much as gurlz Worry
about bazooms. They are often seen flexing the part
of their arm where the biceps are supposed to be and

then examining the critical area with magnifying glasses, X-ray machines, ultrasound scanners Etck in search of missing muscles.

I do exactly the same thing in my bazoom area of course. But just as gurlz are bullied into the bazoom hunt by pictures of impossible knockers in magazines, so boyz are encouraged in the muscle hunt by Boyz hero figures in comix who have biceps the size of El Chubb's head. Of course, everybody has biceps of some kind, otherwise yr arms wld just hang floppily down yr shoulders like a long scarf. But on the whole, Gurlz and Boyz can both do without them.

Anyway, V. Muscly blokes often become musclebound and suffer an early banana, so Boyz, if you lack a bicep or two, do not Worry. You will be welcome in bicepless arms of Bazoomless Chubb.

It is V. Revealing to *moi* how concerned a lot of the boyz are about all this stuff.

Have found out two other main thingz:

1) Most Boyz think they ought to fight, if there's a war.
2) They hate the idea of war as much as I do.

So much for the violent sex then. Are blokes just more often violent than gurlz because they are stronger? Or because they get drunk more often?

7 pm. Have not spoken to Basil for three daze. Why? Where is he?

7.35 pm. Will NOT ring him.

7.40 pm. He should ring ME.

7.42 pm. Anyway, if I ring him, he'll be out and it will make *moi* feel werse.

7.44 pm. Maybe the phone's off the hook.

7.46 pm. I'll just try 1471, in case he phoned and I didn't hear. Sometimes you don't hear the phone even though you've been sitting next to it for a few hours. You can just go into a sort of daze when you don't hear it properly, I think.

7.48 pm. Oh, well, someone did ring, about five hours ago. But they withheld their number. That was prob him, then, forgetting I'd still be at school. So that's fine, I can ring.

I ring.

'Hello.' (milk chocolate, liquid choccy, liquid FUDGE)

'Splffftgzgt. Basil! You're in!'

'No. This is Junior.'

'Oh.'

'D'you want Basil?'

'Splffftgz mssh plooomb.'

'Eh?'

'Yes please.' (he's there, he's there)

'I'll see if he's in.' (he's not there, he's not there)

Usual loud clunky sounds of whirring, shouting Etck.

'Hello.' (is it him?)

'Mffffsplggnttt. Basil?'

'Yes? Who is it?' (it's him!)

'Me.'

'Who?'

'Me. L . . . sppplgnttzflm . . . Letty.'

'Oh. Letty. Darling. How are you?'

'Fine.'

'Lovely. Must meet up really soon.' (he loves me. I knew it)

'How about tomorrow?'

'Er.'

'Or Saturday?' (he must know it's Valentine's Day coming up, he must)

'Look. It's still a bit difficult with work. What about next week?'

'It's half-term. We're away. Please, Basil. I must see you. Can I see you Sunday the 21st?' (I can't berleeve I am doing this.)

'Sure. Why not. Great. See you then.'

'Yes. Darling.'

I blow him a kiss. Am I going mad?

x x x x x x

Fri Feb 12

More interviews with boyz. Pluck up courage to ask Josef. He sez yes. Make a date to do it on first day after half-term. Feel incredibly nervous, but V. Pleased to have made contact. Must do some research. Do not want to let him down.

Off early from skule so go to interview Daniel. Just a few little short tiny months ago I'd have spent five daze Worrying about seeing him. I remember how I swooned over his hair the colour of wet sand at sunset and his eyes like blue Smarties. Now, when he saunters over, running a slender mitt through his wig, I notice only his slight squint and the V. Large pluke on his chin. His eyes are luking more like wine gums today (red and sticky) and his hair is oddly lank, more like mangrove swamp at midnite. How fickle is the eye of love, or something.

Daniel feels it wld be his duty to fight if called. He fancies himself as a pilot. Have to admit he wld luke V. Gude in Biggles-style helmet, but pretend I don't think so and ask, wld he be happy bombing innocent civilians?

'In order to make an omelette, Letty,' he sez pompously, 'you must break eggs.'

All right, all right, I know that. Granny Chubb told me.

Decide to interview Kurt Flasher and Saul Spangle together.

Saul sez all soldiers should wear lilac uniforms, it would make them kinder. Am V. Interested in this notion and feel cld do whole film on colour therapy. But Kurt scoffs in irritation. Kurt comes from a military family. All his ancestors appear to be generals, brigadiers Etck so they prob think he is a bit of a wuss, going in for a film course. As if trying to prove he is big tough guy in the family tradition, Kurt sez that boyz these daze have no sense of responsibility, or community, cos they have no wars to fight. The only way, he thinks, for boyz to 'grow up' wld be to do National Service which wld stop them being moaning whingeing drug addicts and give them a taste of 'real life'. Would he like to do that himself then?

No, he didn't need to, himself. It's for other people.

Surprise, surprise. So glad he has got his interesting film on big tough darts players to be getting on with.

Sneak off for coffee with Saul, who sez that the wood that used to be used to make the bows for violins came from trees that were also used to dye soldiers' uniforms red. Hmmn. Intriguing mix of war and peace there. Maybe shld call film *Melody or Mayhem: The Choice*. And open with shots of trees, swaying in wind, then being felled. Violins? Or violence? Sounds V. Channel 4.

Midnight: Why did soldiers used to always wear red? Surely wld just make them better targets.

2 am. Horrible dream of Josef in red suit, at barbers. The barber produces vast shears and cuts Josef's head off. This war stuff really getting to me. V. Glad it's half-term.

Sat Feb 13
SAD-ON-SEA COUNTDOWN: 2 DAYS

Cannot help feeling V. Glad we are not travelling today, as it is the 13th, but know if we were it wld be V. Good for quelling my superstition. If we got there safely (arg, grone, panick) then it wld prove there is nothing wrong with 13. You only notice the 13th if something V. Bad happens on it. But of course V. Bad things happen on every date (at least, this is wot I tell self. Must find cure for superstition. Wonder if hypnosis wld be the answer? Or maybe just Growing Up, getting a Life Etck wld do the trick).

I am V. Glad also that we are going to lurvely, cosy, home-from-home in Sad-on-Sea, instead of horrible thrusting foreign holiday where nobody is happy.

10.30 pm. Feel V. Glumey after doing Valentine's Week quiz in *Smirk*:

Scored 9 out of 36.

The scores went like this:

> 30—36 You will have a scorching Valentine's day, in fact, you don't NEED Valentine's day, your whole life is one big Valentine's day!
>
> 25—30 Hmm. Hot stuff. Could be a BIGGY round the corner.
>
> 20—25 Winsome, but charming. You'll get your man in the end if you play your cards right.
>
> 15—20 Never mind, better luck next year.

Then they stopped.

I did the quiz again, trying to luke on the brighter side and answering the questions positively, with what I think politicians call 'being economical with the truth.'

I scored 11.

Am never buying *Smirk* again.

Anyway. Tomorrow is Sunday, so there won't be any Valentine's cards anyway.

Unless they're hand delivered.

Sun Feb 14
St Valentine's Day, Worry, Worry . . . Panick!
COOKING, GRANNY CHUBB

8 am. Yippee! Massive, exquisite, ravishing, lacey, gorgeous Valentine propped against door.

151

My heart leaps up like laughing dolphin...

...and plunges down like glumey porpoise

It is a vast plush card with one of those V. Romantic satin hearts edged with frills. And scented! Oooooooh. My heart leaps up like leaping dolphin.

8.10. Have just read message:

> *My love for you is stronger*
> *than steel or stone or iron*
> *It comes to you with loads*
> *And loads of LOVE from?*

My heart plops back like glumey porpoise. What a completely naff card it is, after all. (Well, it could be from Basil, but even my imagination cannot stretch Basil to rhyme with iron).

Can't Brian see that I just DON'T CARE and NEVER WILL?

Mon Feb 15
George Washington's Birthday, USA
SAD-ON-SEA

When I'm away from SAD-ON-SEA, I forget how much I lurve it. Then, when I get there again, I think, is there any place on Earth more lovely than lovely, glumey, chilly, windy, wet, grey, rocky, lonesome, drab SAD-ON-SEA? I lurve the pale pebbly beach, the grey stormy sea, the cawing old gulls. I lurve the little tea shoppes with their little hard rock cakes. I lurve the little sticks of rock with SAD-ON-SEA written all the way through. I lurve to think of the little woole shoppe with the yellow cellophane over the window so that the wool doesn't fade in the watery sun that occasionally shines through the little woole shoppe's little windowe. I lurve the SAD-ON-SEA Antique shoppe, with its cluttered window full of dead flies, old lead soldiers, Noddy figures and a one-eyed bear.

Oh to be in SAD-ON-SEA
now that Feb is there
your wavy waves
your pebbly shores
your little one-eyed bear . . .

Think maybe I cld get job writing rhymes for cards to sell in nice little shops in nice little SAD-ON-SEA, instead of trying to ingratiate self into gharstly high-speed cut throat werld of film industry Etck.

Benjy V. Keen to buy anciente lead soldier. Dad was thrilled and said he and his brothers used to have one, which they shared. Thort he only had old dented cake tin to play with. But he had a whole lead soldier! Obviously his childhood not as deprived as he makes out.

Mother puts foot down re lead soldier – lead poisoning Etck. But Benjy does not mind; that is

155

what is so great about SAD-ON-SEA: things that wld cause big row at home ('Must have soldier. Will scream and scream hed off until soldier in pocket' Etck) just don't seem to happen in magical werld of SAD-ON-SEA.

Instead of screaming and wailing, Benjy gazes thoughtfully at the dead flies: 'Aren't flies lucky? They can go wherever they like. They can go to the cinema for nothing. And get into 12s.'

Maybe this is wot it was like in the Fifties, when families had little and were V. Happy and stayed together.

Tue Feb 16
Shrove Tuesday
Chinese New Year.
PANCAKE DAY!
SAD-ON-SEA

Apparently, for the Chinese, this is Year of the Hare. Must ask Lotus if this means you get V. Hairy if born in this year or else can jump well. Or maybe just have V. Long ears. Wonder what Lotus thinks of Chinese in Tibet?

Wonder wot we all think

of horrible things our grate nations have done in our name?

Wonder if I DARE interview Josef?

V. Bracing walk along shore from SAD-ON-SEA all the way to Little Puddledcan and back.

Mother made pancakes with Benjy. Cannot remember her making pancakes before. We celebrate with whole lemon and half a bag of sugar. We eat delicious crispy (quite burnt, actually) pancakes by roaring coal fire. Read a lot more *War and Peace*. Am really getting into this marvellous buke. Shows how gude a holiday can be for the brane.

Wed Feb 17
Ash Wednesday
SAD-ON-SEA

Go luking for crabs. Do not get any, but get small jam jar of tadpoles. Dad is over-the-mune.

Strange to think that Adored Father, who dives headfirst into bottles of Old Bastard lager at any opportunity, curses Werld for failing to appreciate his Massive Talent Etck, totters around on emotional highwire with unscrupulous Trapeze Artiste and all this, shld be so happy with jamjar of tadpoles. This is the Strange Magick of Sad-on-Sea. This is how he spent his own childhood Etck. I thort he was stuck in inner-city slum and never saw fresh air or a crab

(except at the doctors). But who am I to moan?
Probably he went to seaside once or twice on free
working men's education trip for poor families Etck.

Thur Feb 18
SAD-ON-SEA

Another fabulous day at fabulous SAD-ON-SEA.
Mother and Father walk tenderly arm-in-arm or sit
like cosy marrows in front of cosy fire. We have had
cream teas every day and I think my nose has put on
a little bit of weight. But who cares? No distracting
boyz in lurvely SAD-ON-SEA.

Fri Feb 19
SAD-ON-SEA

Wander lonesome as a cloud by lonesome shore
thinking of fudge-coloured wig . . . But even Basil's
absence cannot detract from glories of vast
tumultuous sky and ever-changing yet constant
ocean. In fact, only think that he, like *moi*, is just tiny
dot spinning in cosmos . . .

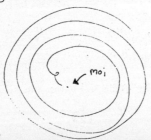

Sat Feb 20

Interesting Fact: John Glenn became first American Astronaut on this day in 1962. Fancy, and him still going up in Space as recently as 1999!

Home via Granny Gosling's gaff – her birthday.

We do our best to be nice.

We sit down to tea with scary thin cups, saucers, milk jugs, spoons and other items unknown to 21st century Teenage Worrier. My mother and I fix Benjy with beady looks, dreading inevitable crash. G. Gosling had made tissue-paper-thin cucumber sandwiches.

'Ooh. Cubumber. Lubbly,' shouts Benjy, taking six at once in mistake for one.

Benjy has made a birthday card out of old loo rolls and dried beans. I dread the Gosling's response. I am right.

'Ooooh Benjy. AREN'T you the CLEVER one!

He's so artistic, like his mother! But darling, is this a joke?' (*Benjy has written: 'To DeAr GraNbUm'*)

To DeAr GraNbUm

'I don't think that's very funny. Oh of course, he's dyslexic, aren't you, darling? Not your fault. Lots of very very clever and famous people have been dyslexic. But they MUST be sent to the right schools. You're not sending him to that dreadful Sluggs, are you daaarling?'

'Um,' blushes my mother. 'I'd prefer NOT to, but . . .'

'What Alice means is that we can't afford a fee-paying school,' says my father briskly. 'But if Sluggs is good enough for Letty . . .'

'Oh, but it isn't, is it Letty? Poor little thing. Well, not so little. Is it cold up there? Teee heee har di har.'

There is a nasty crunching sound. Benjy has bitten off a bit of cup.

'Spit it out. Spit it out. Quick!' My mother is hysterical.

Benjy milks the moment by looking as if he is about to swallow. Father attempts to prise his mouth open. Benjy, seemingly in shock, keeps jaws firmly clamped. After 45 seconds he calmly opens gob. Mother nervously extracts two pieces of china from rosy gums of Benjy and, hands shaking, fits them neatly into gap in cup. Perfect fit.

'He can't have swallowed any then,' gasps Father, hyperventilating.

'Eat lots of bread,' squeaks Mother. Benjy eats remaining six sandwiches in one go.

I am famished. Have only had one which wld not keep mayfly alive.

'Poor Little Benjy. Trust it's not a sign of some visual impairment, dear,' murmurs Granny Gosling. 'Well, I mushn't keep you,' she hums, vacuuming her third tumbler of sherry.

'But you haven't opened the presents yet,' says my Only Mother, crestfallen.

'Oh, I like to keep them till later.'

I hate it when people do this. You go to all the trouble of choosing cards and wrapping things up and getting sellotape in your wig and then they don't even bother to look.

'You musht come again soon. Perhaps when Leonard's dishcovered the gene for making a living. Daaarling Leonard, jusht a joke. How's the novel going? Got to chapter one yet? Har ti he ti heee har ti he ti heee har ti he ti heee.'

 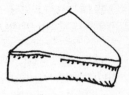

Why chalk and CHEESE?

Why not chalk and CHESS PIECE?

Or cheese and CHOCOLATE?

Sun Feb 21
COOKING, GRANNY CHUBB

Lovely to see G. Chubb and well-fed Rover again. Oh joy. My two grannies are chalk and cheese. One never says anything nice, the other never says anything nasty.

Thinks: Why chalk and cheese? Why not chalk and chocolate? Or chessboard and cheese? Chalk and cheese aren't so very unlike each other when you think about it. I bet some cheese would make a mark on a blackboard and you can crumble them both and they're a similar colour, too. In fact some of that posh cheese from the Fromagerie that Only Mother visits once a year is V like chalk. Tis thorts like these that take up so much space in brane of El Chubb and detract from useful stuff that will gain me place in thrusting reel werld, I fear . . .

Granny Chubb teaches me how to cook meringues, kool.

Hang out with Hazel. She has not told her parents the whole truth and still seems V. Low. They have been as kind as they can be, but they just don't really understand the pressure Hazel is under at her posh skule. They have rallied round and got her three private tutors. They are obviously akshully made entirely of money. But they don't seem to understand that really this is more pressure for Haze. I mean, you feel much MORE of a failure if you fail despite all the privlidges money can buy, doncha?

Also, she is still missing Mandy badly. I HATE Mandy. How could she DO this when Hazel ran away for her? Wish I could introduce Hazel to someone else but I don't know any other lesbians apart from my Mum's frendz Viv'n'Joyce.

Or I don't know if I do. They're not likely to pin notices round their necks at Sluggs. Akshully, there must be loads of lesbians at Sluggs, as it's V. Common. Maybe I shld put a notice up?

Might be disapproved of by skule Thought Police of course, it's not been so long since skuleteachers were even forbidden by the Govt to mention lesbians and gays in a positive manner. Imagine trying to ban talking about so many people's preferred way of life, and at the same time go on about how terrible Communism was for trying to control attitudes Etck! Inconsistent, or what? Am def. going to launch campaign to say gays are as normal as anyone else. After all it is more common to be gay than to have red hair (though not more common than acne).

Anyway, I doubt if Hazel wld like to be advertised just yet, while heart still broken. Will ask her.

Spend afternoon dressing, undressing, redressing Etck for Basil.

Hazel helpful in vague sort of way. 'Blokes are such a drag, wanting you luking like 44-inch lovely Mandy Mammaries, an uninhibited rocket scientist and lapdancer from Dagenham. Why don't you just stay natural?'

Natural for Hazel is one thing. Natural for El Chubb, quite another, I tell her.

Natural for Hazel is one thing. For El Chubb, quite another...

Midnight. This has been best evening of my Life.

Candle-lit supper in exotick Lebanese restaurant. YESSS!

Waiter whisking back and forth with an armoury of cutlery. In romantick dim light, tried to eat ravishing-luking item prepared to resemble gorgeous yellow flower, only to discover it was my folded napkin in a glass. That's the kind of thing they do in places like this, it's very classy.

Couldn't understand a single word of the menu so fluttered fake lashes so skittishly one shot off and landed in soup of smarmy-luking middle-aged man out with giggly young woman whose glass he kept refilling as she got gigglier. He was gazing soulfully into her big bue eyes and big brash cleavage with alternate gazes, and didn't seem to have noticed it. Shouldn't cause any complications then, unless he has a V. Suspicious Wife (who this person almost certainly isn't) who takes X-ray pix of his stomach while he's asleep.

Whispered to Basil to order for *moi*.

'This all looks fine, what you have here,' he told the waiter, 'but it's for the Brits, isn't it? Just imagine you're at home. Why don't you give us what you'd give your friends? I know Beirut well, great town.'

Wow. Fancy going to a restaurant and ignoring the menu, that's really something.

The waiter looked quite pleased and went away.

'I didn't know you'd been to . . . to . . .

Beetroot . . .' sez *moi*, a bit dubiously.

'Beirut. A business trip. Another beautiful city ravaged by man's inhumanity to man.'

'Where is it exactly?'

'It's . . . er . . . in the . . . um . . . er, Lebanon of course.'

'War is terrible, isn't it?' sez I, originally, cringe, shrink Etck.

'It is, Letty, but because we allow it to be. Most of us stand by and wring our hands. A few get involved, to bring these terrible things to an end for ever.' He luked at me with a long, meaningful luke I did not understand the meaning of.

Then the waiter showed up, carrying about three hundred V. Small plates of things that luked like grey baked beans, stuff you find in the lawn-mower, and little fried things like they have in Nugget-U-Like.

'Wot is all this?' I asked Basil, trying to sound enthusiastic.

He waved his arms about vaguely. 'Specialities of the region,' he said. 'Wonderful stuff. Imbibe! Consume!'

Noticed next table now complaining about spider in soup and tried to keep low profile, which with my bazooms is not difficult. Noticed also to surprise of *moi* that Basil was luking at the food with luke rather like the way I felt, and not eating much.

'Bit off my appetite,' he said, smiling tenderly at *moi*. 'Maybe I only have room for one exquisite sensation at a time.'

Eeechawawa! He sez the most wonderful thingz! Still luking tenderly at *moi*, he swirls wine about in glass and then sniffs it before drinking it Etck, in authentick posh fashione – this is the kind of thing that sends Granny Gosling into pirouetting ecstasies. The wineglass was so long and thin and classy that unfortunately he was not able to drink out of it whilst still fixing me with swimmingly romantick gaze, and was forced to tip his head back to luke at ceiling instead, during which key moment El Chubb was able to sweep large dollop of grey baked beans that had landed in lap on to floor. Smarmy luking bloke at next table stepped straight in it whilst standing authoritatively up to continue spider-in-soup dispute with waiter, but fortunately this also luked like a mishap that wouldn't be revealed until he began to take a few steps across the posh carpet.

Basil kept stroking my knee under the table. I had no idea the knee was such an erogenous zone. Have strong feeling that whole of *moi* is erogenous zone when Basil is nigh . . . Wot with that and two glasses of wine it was V. Difficult to concentrate on exotick baked beans, lawn-mowings Etck.

The grate thing about Basil, is that he is really really into serious issues. He has a raging hatred of the Brit clarse system, just like *moi*, and wants a werld where everyone is equal. He thinks that the internet is the big way to bring people together. He is NOT just in it for the money. He also hints at some much more Important Work, that must remain

Secret, but that is for Werld peace.

Oh, at last I have met a kindred spirit, who is not only as handsome as the morning, but is brave, noble, Etck Etck.

Best thing of all, is, although he will be away working a lot in next few weeks, he will be around for the whole of the Easter hols. Oh joy unconfined. Ask to interview him about war, before he goes, for my film. He loves the idea. He's coming over on Tuesday. He is my boyfrend, obviously. I am seeing him nearly every day.

Tiddley umpetty tiddley de
I lurve Baz and he lurves me
Tiddley widdley diddley bume
can't wait to get him up here in my rume
Plinketty plinketty bumledy dum
Himmetty hertitty hummety hum.

Basil flicks casually through array of shiny plastick in his wallet, about as many ways of paying for The Gude Life as a pack of playing cards. But in the end he puts the cash down on the table.

'You can't beat the Real Thing,' he sez, putting arm around my waist and slipping his hand around to my front just ever so slightly. Aaaargh! I wonder if absence of rounded object at this point will have put him off for ever?

No. He is different. You can't beat the Real Thing.

Mon Feb 22

7 am. Shtupid. Clock.

7.10. Why won't it go quiet?

7.15. Clock shmock clockketty clock. Go way shtupid clock.

7.20. Arg. Perluke. It is a skule day. Have got a lot of little woolly caps on my teeth. My tongue has swollen to five times its usual size and is made of sandpaper. There is a flock of owls playing bongo in my hed, which has a metal band round it. Someone is tightening the metal band.

Will never drink alcohol ever again.

8.30 am. Stole some fizzy stuff of Dad's and stuck face in sink full of cold water for five mins.

Feel grate. What a grate night last night. Skippetty weee.

NB new werd: imbibe. Amazing – had the memory to luke it up after last night, but such is the power of Basil to drill into my brane. Anyway, it means 'to drink'. Will take vow to limit imbibing.

Have also discovered nice new werd for being drunk: **swacked**. Was totally swacked last night due to over-imbibing of certain shubshtances, but am now firmly under the affluence of inkahol again, like orl writers. (**NB: Affluence** means being wealthy. Three new werds in one paragraph! Is this a record? No it's a CD, arf, arf).

8.30 pm. Interviewed Josef and Brian today.

I met Josef in the caff. I was flustered, furious with myself for having hangover and wished I hadn't organized to do Brian only half an hour later.

Josef was very quiet and very troubled, as I knew he would be. His English is not bad. He stutters. There were long silences when we both just stared at the table. He told me about his dad being shot. And his little brother, who was only twelve. His brother had hurled a rock at the soldiers and they had shot him dead. Josef said, over and over again, 'Why did I not hurl rock? Why did I not hurl rock?'

I tried to comfort him.

I said he would be dead too if he had.

He said he might as well be. He doesn't know where his mum or his other brother or his sister are. He became very angry and said he would like to strangle his family's murderers very slowly.

I stared at the table some more. Then I said, thinking of Nelson Mandela, might there ever be room for forgiveness?

Josef's fist, which is huge, crashed down on the table. 'Never!'

Then Brian came in.

'Next interview, yes?' growled Josef. And he stormed out.

'OOH, who's got a bee in his bonnet?' quipped Brian, plonking himself down where Josef had been sitting. I tried to adjust the gap in reality. I should have run after Josef of course, but I didn't.

In a funny way, the interview with Brian was even more shocking. I suppose I shld have known what his idea of fighting 'for his country' was.

His fave songs are *Ballad of the Green Berets*, *Tie a Yellow Ribbon round the Old Oak Tree* and *Two Little Boys* by Rolf Harris. Am living in parallel universe to biggest cardigan of all time. However, thought I must try to fathom his reasons more deeply:

'Look, Letty,' he says in his most patronizing manner. 'It is essential to have armies. Without armies, how could there be wars? I mean, righteous wars, of course. Like the Second World War in which we bravely defeated the Nazis.'

Can't argue with that. Especially as mind flicks back to that awful film of Auschwitz . . .

'But what other righteous wars have there been?'

'The one right now.'

'Don't you think it's a bit cowardly just to bomb people and not go in yourself?'

'Oh, it may be that people say a soldier who is ready to kill, but not ready to die, is a coward. But you must be ready to do both. The trouble with you bleeding heart liberals is you don't see that freedom is a precious thing that must be defended. If necessary by shedding one's own blood.'

Feel a grudging hint of admiration for this view. Put on best Jeremy Paxo style interview manner. 'So, Brian Bolt, you would be ready to do both.'

'Well, naturally, I see myself as more of a strategist. Officer material. People with exceptionally high IQs, like me, would be wasted at the front. I'd probably be a commanding officer, or possibly a code breaker. They wouldn't want me to risk my LIFE.'

'So, er, you think your superior intelligence puts you above other soldiers?'

'Naturally. And those of great intelligence must be preserved, to breed the best possible babies for the next generation. You see, there are hidden benefits to war.'

'Huh?'

'Well, population control.'

'So, Brian Bolt, would you say that war is a good way of ridding us of some thickos in order to make way for brainiacs?'

'Well, yes, to the extent that if we send the stupidest people out to battle, the remaining individuals will be of a higher than average calibre.'

'And, um, would you also apply that to women?'

'The ugly ones, yes. Ha. ha. Not you, though Letty. You're gorgeous.' And then he jumped on me. I always knew he was a nerd, but until this moment I had no idea Brian was more or less a fascist.

'What the hell do you think you're doing?'

'Come on, you know you like it.'

'I do NOT.' I push him off. 'I want our relationship to be strictly platonic. Is that quite clear?'

'What's that mean?'

V. Amazed that Brian 'eight brains' Bolt does not know the meaning of platonic, but am too embarrassed to tell him.

'Look it up,' I storm. And leave.

Brian. Bluerghh.

NB For all of you Teenage Worriers out there who do not know the meaning of 'platonic', it is derived from yr grate philosopher Plato, who talked of perfect, but not carnal, love, ie: that is, NO SEX.

Midnight. Furious with myself for arranging the interviews so close. For having hangover. For having spent whole half-term NOT doing any research . . .

Tue Feb 23
PERIOD DUE

School trip. Yippeee. We are going with Mr Cantanker, the crazed Technology teacher. How lurvely, he is taking us to the highly edukational widget workshop and museum. And I have my period. Ooh, lucky me. I love having my lovely period when I have to spend several hours in a museum with only one loo and a lovely skule coach with no loos at all. Lucky, lucky me.

'Why do we have a widget workshop and museum?' asks Chlamydia Clutterbuck, her fountain pen poised, her brow eagerly furrowed in the bliss of learning. 'Stoppit Zelda!' She aims savage kick at poor old Zelda who is away with the fairies as usual and has started fiddling with Chlamydia's hair.

'We have a workshop and museum for widgets,' yawns the group leader, 'because it is no use for a job-seeker having a widget unless he or she knows how best to first make it and then use it to its full capacity. That goes for gizmos too. We are proud of our British widgets and gizmos but most proud of our thingumajigs, which are the world's finest, let me just move you on to this astounding example of thingumajig manufacture . . . see the shiny knobs, gleaming spindles, exquisite throddles . . . drone . . . drone . . . in fact, without home-crafted thingumajigs, where would British Industry be? We would not even have the humble paperclip.'

The humble paperclip! Our hearts overflow with excitement and joy. We skip merrily about.

'The humble paperclip?' I ask. 'Would we also be short of bath plugs? Staplers? And wonderful wonderful tins of British peas? If we didn't have widgets?'

'Yes, yes.'

Oh, joy . . . Wot is the use of a werld without interesting widgets, tins of peas and bath plugs, and wonderful humble paperclips, eh?

Our group leader sees that he has lost the

advantage. 'Who would like to throddle a widget spindle?'

'Yippee.' It is our hearts' desire.

'You look like a sensible gurl,' says the group leader to Zelda's bust. 'Why don't you have the first go?'

Zelda skips vaguely in the direction of the widget spindle and before we can shout 'NO' she has pressed sixteen buttons and is swinging far above our heads on the end of a throddle.

Zelda's helper, who had snuck off for a quick fag, runs forward, ashen faced: 'ZELDA! COME DOWN THIS MINUTE!'

'I am Rose, I am Rose on the *Titanic*. Where oh where is Leonardo?' sings Zelda. She is having a lovely time. Unfortunately the throddle, Zelda in its grasp, has a mind of its own and is now marching up a series of wires and pulleys towards something that lukes very much like a crocodile mating with a cement-mixer.

With gharstly jackal-like cackles, the group leader, the helper and Cantanker all leap upon the widget and press levers and buttons and pull pullies with wild abandone. The throddle carrying Zelda speeds up a fraction and rotates: CLANKETTY CLANKETTY CLANKETTY SPROINGG.

'Hang on Zelda!' 'Let go, Zelda!' they cry. It is just as well Zelda never does wot she is told as she is in a werld of her own.

But she is no fule. She can see the mashing metal teeth approaching.

'*Oh, Leo,*' she sings.
If you were only here,
I could save you save you my dearest dear.
But you are not here, or even near.'

Then she does a little curtsey, which is quite an achievement in the circumstances and shouts down, 'It's the fourteenth button on the right.'

I will never trust Cantanker to teach anything ever again. He pushed the thirteenth button. The throddle went into overdrive. The noble helper leapt forward to press the fourteenth button and Zelda swirled gracefully down to the ground.

'Can I ride on the gizmo?' she asked no-one in particular.

The adults needed a sit down after this so we all went to the shop and bought V. Interesting things like widget bookmarks, gizmo pencil sharpeners and stuff. Jack Spriggs got a dozen rubbers for 25p.

Syd Snoggs asked him if he had enough rubbers har har har and Jack Spriggs, without missing a beat said: 'Yeah, but they'd be no good for you, Syd, they don't have teeny weeny sizes.'

As usual, no fudge. What is the point of having museum shops without fudge?

8 pm. Spent usual two hours cleaning humble kitchen before arrival of Baz. Mother twitters about. Notice she has put on lipstick.

11 pm. Interview with Basil was best yet. Swoon, he's so articulate. Talks wonderfully about the corruption of governments all over the werld and how can you be sure any war is worth fighting? Goes on about our own govt giving arms to other countries with one hand and talking about human rights with the other, so to speak. Etck Etck. Brilliant.

'If the werld's governments really wanted it,' he carried on, 'they could stop war tomorrow. But they don't. Our oleaginous so called leaders know there's a fortune in making things to kill people, it's a massive contribution to the economies of the richest nations on earth. Now, if we were prepared to live more simply, that evil business cld be stamped out. Isn't it better to live on bread in a werld without guns, than on caviare in a werld in which thousands of innocent people are killed because the weapons business makes us rich?'

I thought of our candle-lit dinner and wondered if we wld have felt quite the same eating a cheese sandwich in a bus shelter. But these unwerthy thoughts have no place in any conversation with a Yuman Bean of True Nobilitie.

He gazes at *moi* with melting gaze.

'Love is the only antidote to war, Letty. Some

178

people, like me, love children, and animals – all the wild creatures of the forests and lakes – and would die to preserve them from harm. Why? Who knows?' and then he cast his manly eyes to the ceiling, as if looking for an answer there. Benjy has been flicking bubble gum up there as he doesn't like to put it on the floor, where he thinks it will be unhappy. Basil luked momentarily puzzled, but continued in manly tones of suppressed emotion: 'All I know is, that among the peoples of the world, there is one universal saying I hold true: *If you encounter a human and a cobra ready to strike, kill the human first.*'

Phew. He said loads more, most of which I didn't understand. But I know it will impress Alfonsa. As will the old cleft chin, fudge-coloured wig and so on . . .

When the tape has stopped running, Basil takes my hand and whispers in my ear to avoid attracting attention of Adored Father who keeps crashing noisily in and out.

'We have to be warriors for peace, Letty. There aren't very many of us who care. But I know a few who do. We're in regular contact. You've been helping us, without knowing it. They're very special people, who want a better werld. Like you. Are you with us?' I just have time to gasp 'um' before Adored Father crashes in again. Results in no kissing opportunities, tragickally.

Managed a quick one at the front door.

I think I am getting addicted.

1 am. New werd: oleaginous. Means oily or greasy. Wot a grate werd. Wot a grate mind. Basil: fude for soul and body. Phwooor.

Wed Feb 24
BABYSIT

In RE, Miss Dawgkoller gives us a little sermon on happiness. She cheers us up by telling us about all the children in the world who are blown to bits, have no food Etck. So what have we got to complain about? Tells us, always better to luke on bright side, say

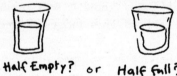

glass is half full rather than half empty Etck. I glance across at Josef, who is, as usual, drawing.

'Wot if glass is full of cyanide?' whispers Aggy.

'Share your thoughts with the rest of us, Agatha,' smirks Miss Dawgkoller.

Aggy shuffles. 'What if the glass is full of poison? Miss?' she mutters.

'That is a perfect illustration of teenage pessimism,' hisses Miss Dawgkoller. 'Exactly what teenagers today are too prone to. If you can't BE happy, you can at least LOOK happy. If you want a job, you want to look bright, cheerful, bushy tailed.' (I have visions of merry tinkling laughter of flock of foxes being pursued to their banana by horde of hounds with Portillo's face.) 'And now,' continues the Dawgkoller, 'let me give you a little hint. Say one short word before entering a room for an interview, or ringing up about a job. Say "thrush". This will conjure up a Good Image. A Good Image of a cheerful little bird. It will also compose your face in a lovely smile. Try it.'

Unfortunately, we have just been learning about STDs and other diseases of the underbits in PSE. To us, 'thrush' does not immediately bring to mind a charming birdy. In fact, must admit I am not sure what this birdy is supposed to look like. Cld recognize robin, probably, and pigeon. Also, parrot.

Me and Spiggy and Aggs spent twenty minutes in loos trying to say 'thrush' in way Dawgkoller suggests, larfing too much to see if it werks. But, weirdly, although you'd think 'cheese' wld be better, it makes you look V. Cheesy, whereas 'thrush' said all brightly, gives you a kind of eager, I'll-do-anything-for-you luke. Wonder if Dawgkoller uses this method before entering classrume. She always comes in smirking alarmingly.

Thur Feb 25

Interesting Fact: Well, quite interesting, espesh as birds are big subject this week. Christopher Wren (wren is a bird, for all you urban Teenage Worriers who've never seen a sheep), who built St Pauls cathedral (that's the V. Big domed one you can't see V. Well in London) died today in 1723. Wonder if he wld have liked the Greenwich Dome?

Can recognize flamingo, too. Akshully, quite pleased with my total bird recognition.

Today was Benjy's skule consultation. Mother as usual banging on about needing more dosh. Wants to send him to posh skule.

I notice this is always happening with middle-class boyz while their sisters go off to skules like Sluggs. Just like me and Ashley, who got paid for by Grandma Gosling before her dosh ran out (she lost it all in some undertaker's, I mean underwriter's, insurance collapse). So unFAIR. Well, if Mum wants Benjy to grow up wrecked, with stiff upper lip, no feelings Etck, she can. Course, if she wants him to be werld leader and expert at blowing people to smithereens then posh skule is probably the right course. It is obvious that World Leaders, Grate Heroes & Heroines Etck often seem to have had V. Grimme childhoods – at least the British ones do –

with mothers swanning in covered in wafts of perfume putting a grape on their pillow before sending them off to boarding skule and refusing to reply to their tear-stained letters begging to be released.

As far as I can see, Benjy is no more dyslexic than *moi*, which may not be saying chum.

Ring Baz six times. Ansaphone.

Fri Feb 26
FILM COURSE

Interesting Fact: Grand National started today in 1839. I spose sport is war without bloodshed, but the Grand National must have killed almost as many horses as ye Charge of ye Light Brigade.

Interviewed Jack Spriggs at lunchtime. He didn't go on about philosophy, ethicks, idealism Etck, which was a bit of a shame, but he told some war jokes instead. I wasn't sure at first if war jokes fitted in my visione of the Grate movie of Men and War, but perhaps it cld be a dramatick contrast, viz:

Officer to Private: Well. Off you go Smith, over the top. Goodbye.
Private: I think I'd prefer to say 'au revoir' sir.
Officer: No, Smith, it's goodbye.

Jack Spriggs carried on thus:

'Nah. Don't fancy war. Too noisy and you wouldn't want to be seen dead with some of the people.'

'If bombing's a good way to end a war, let's blow up the planet.'

'Who'll be right when nobody's left?'

'Oh, Yeah. One of me ancestors fell at Waterloo. Got pushed off the platform.'

'Who was that bloke who won? Duke Ellington?'

'You know what kind of a person you've got to be to be buried with military honours? Dead.'

'I don't think governments should have wars, they should leave it up to families.'

''Course, battleground's no place fer cowards. I'd prove that by runnin' fer me life.'

He didn't seem to be taking this V. Serious Matter seriously. Or maybe he was. But I like Jack Spriggs.

Alfonsa is V. Pleased with me.

She watched all my rough footage today. She larfed her hed off at Brian and also at Jack, though for different reasons.

'Gharstly pompous eeengleesh pratt' (Brian), 'nice cheeeky chappy' (Jack). 'So sweeeet.'

She was silent through Josef. Her jaw dropped. But it dropped more for Basil, who I saved till last.

'Oooh. So eloquent! So chaarrming! So truthful! So RIGHT!' she applauded. And so gorgeous, I could see her thinking.

184

She even let me hang on to the video camera for a week more.

'Why not? Eeeet only seeet heerre wasting eet's life otherwise.'

She thinks I shld go out and about and do 'vox pops' with boyz on the street. Suggests I take one of the blokes on the film course, so I won't be done for soliciting. 'Ow abowt Stanleeeeee?'

If she only knew.

'No,' I squeak. 'Will you?' I turn desperately to Oliver Auteur.

'I don't mind. I'll do one day interviewing with you if you do one day for me.'

'Wonderfoool,' sez Alfonsa, brimming over with joy at collaboration. Wot a releef. Stanley is luking rounder and quieter than ever, but V. Red. With luck, someone will take him for a tomato and douse him in vinaigrette. Arrange to meet Oliver at 8 am tomorrow and tour London's mean streets. His own film project is V. Boring actually, following a day in the life of an accountancy firm, but I have a feeling he may have deep imagination waiting to leap out and snare us all with unfathomable depths.

Midnight. Gave in and rang Baz. Sez, he can see me on Sunday.

Isn't last day in February Special?

Sat Feb 27

Amazing. Alarm went off at 7.15 and El Chubb got out of snoring house by 7.25. Left note:

Think this shows new, self-assured, independent *moi*. Why shld I ask every time I go out of the door?

Meet Oliver at tube. Decide to hang around station and accost likely-looking youths. Here are some of our enlightening exchanges:

'Excuse me, I was wondering . . .'

'Bloody hell, if I was selling a body like that, I wouldn't want to video it as well.'

'I'm not selling my body, I'm trying to interview you!'

'I'm not buying your body, I'm asking how much

you'll pay me to take it away, har har har.'

'Excuse me, I was wondering . . .'

'You one of them anoraksics?'

'If you'd . . .'

'You can 'ave a bit of bubble gum if you like.'

'No, I'm . . .'

'This your bloke? You want to feed 'er up a bit, mate, you're going ter cut yerself on the corners.'

'Excuse me, I was wondering . . .'

'Your aura confirms it. The world has lost its sense of wonder, that's the reason why we're all going to burn in hell. But there is A Way. I am a member of the Kiwi Flower Enlightened Path movement of Tooting Bec, and I can see that you'd like to . . .'

'Sorry, mistook you for somebody else . . .'

'Excuse me, I was wondering . . .'

'Ooh. Is it a survey? Carlton loves surveys, don't you Carlton. They always get him to do surveys cos he looks well ard. Go on, Carlton, tell her about how you've shagged everyone in your school and fathered eight babies by the time you was twelve.'

At this point Oliver stepped in in a manful way. 'Look. We're asking serious questions about war. Do you want to answer or not?'

'Oh. War. Nah. Dun' 'appen 'ere, does it, so bollocks to the lot of 'em, uncivilized bastards.'

And off they sloped.

We went for a coffee.

'We need a more direct approach,' said Oliver. 'Let's ask what they think of the Current Situation.'

I think we shld just follow the same recipe as I thought of for crime: 'Hello. You've won the lottery. To qualify, you need to answer a few simple questions.'

It is V. Depressing doing surveys. The next time some poor hopeful person approaches *moi* with a clipboard I will try to be nicer.

By midday the sky, which had been quite a nice foggy grey like Sluggs blazers, was now like midnite and rain gushed down in sheets. No-one on streets.

'Let's try the buses,' said Oliver, still chirpy.

No-one on buses, except knackered mothers with sticky toddlers and pensioners riding round and round on their free bus passes. Felt, couldn't go home, as wld lose face. Oliver suggested a film. So we snuck naughtily into cinema. There were three army recruiting ads.

'Hey,' whispered Olly. 'You could use some of that. You know. Get tough. Make decisions. And intercut it with blank dozy blokes who can't decide which flavour crisps they want.'

Olly is nobody's fule.

10.30 pm. Feel at least something has been salvaged from wreckage of day. Must catch up on Beauty sleep, ahem.

Will try 'thrush' trick out, tomorrow, on Basil. It is last day in February and I Have a Plan . . .

Sun Feb 28

LAST DAY IN FEB – LEAP YEAR! I CAN PROPOSE!
COOKING, GRANNY CHUBB

Am meeting Basil today. Can hardly wait.

12.30. Cooking with G. Chubb.
We do boiled eggs. I tell her we have done it before but she tells me that no-one could have eaten my boiled egg unless at gunpoint and that it is a waste of eggs unless you do it right. Think of the old eggs Benjy uses in potions with wave of guilt at reckless use of resources and wot-hope-is-there-for-future-of-mankind Etck.

2 pm. Yippeeeee. Dad has taken Benjy off to play football in park. He is V. Worried Benjy has no interest in football and will turn into un-sporty nerd without proper fathering. 'If he went to a better school,' snarled Only Mother, 'he'd have proper competitive sports. It's money we need, not outings to the park.'

I am getting V. Worried about my mother's obsession with money. She used to think about the Higher Things in Life, like Art Etck. Now she just whinges every time we ask for a fiver.

Still, with Benjy and Dad out of way, have now got whole afternoon to tart self up for Basil . . . Mother is very keen on Basil. As much to do, I fear, with his fudge-coloured wallet as his fudge-coloured wig. Sometimes wonder if she wld just sell her children to the highest bidder?

Anyway, now for languorous bath, exfoliation, wig wash Etck Etck.

2.10 pm. Just approaching bathrume when violent banging and crashing on door and violent rolling and crashing of thunder and lightning outside usher in dripping weeping Benjy and limping father.

Mother assumes doting motherly luke she reserves solely for Benjy. 'Poor darling. What happened?'

'I've broken my leg, that's what's happened,' roars Only Father.

'He's soaked. Didn't you take his coat?'

Realize demand for Benjy to have a hot bath so he won't get pneumonia is luming so barricade self inside only to discover bath blocked up with disgusting stuff.

'Benjy! WHAT have you been putting in the bath? I'm going to meet the man of my dreams.'

''S only a potion. Has he got a gun?'

'What do you mean? ONLY a potion? What's IN IT?'

I don't know if any of you, dear fellow Teenage Worriers, have ever tried to get a five-year-old to clean the bath. It's easier to do it yourself, even if it is a potion. The potion, Benjy informed me, was only coffee grounds, tea bag, vanilla essence, shampoo and slugs.

'SLUGS??'

'Ony one slug.'

After fumigating the bath, pour in *caresse d'amour* bath oil then realize can't wash wig in oily water. Wash in sink with *Shimmer of a Glimmer* chestnut shampoo. This shld make wig a lovely conker colour and V. Shiny like billiard ball. Get crick in neck. Plunge into lukewarm bath with potato slices on peepers (couldn't find cucumber) and mud mask on mug.

Doorbell rings four times.

Then loud battering.

Stumble down and open door in towel (well, door not actually in towel, you know what I mean). Man at door runs away screaming.

Surge back into bath, screaming at Benjy, father and mother. How come no-one ever answers door? Feel omens for date with Basil are not auspicious.

Peel off mud. Luke a bit flushed, cheeks purplish, like radishes. Chin like postbox. Nose eerie bluish tinge. Odd white patches. Maybe I could get a job as Union Jack. Rub potato slices over cheeks in attempt to kule down complexion. Lucky I got that green foundation that's supposed to reduce 'high colour'.

Dither over whether to use mascara that makes lashes double the thickness or double the length. Why not both? Hmmmm. V. Thick. But not many individual lashes. Uh. Has just stuck them all together in one big lump. Still, my four thick eyelashes are now V. Long, so could be worse.

Decide, ice pink for lips. No, too tarty. Ruby. Too tarty. Horrible dark brown one what looks vile in the tube aksherlly looks better on smacker. Hmmm.

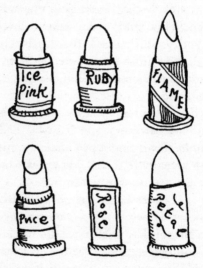

Huh! Think will invent spotty lipstick to match face...

Maybe cld be beauty consultant. Face now greyish. Dab bits of ruby lipstick on cheeks and rub in well. Light frosting on eyelids, upper cheekbone, tip of chin.

This has taken one and a half hours.

Pluke. Am obv allergic to ruby lipstick as cheeks

now flusher than ever. Scrub hard, more green foundation. Turn out entire bathrume and find some fake tan. Dab little bit over green. No difference.

Concentrate on wig. Spend three quarters of an hour attempting hairdresser style blow dry by pulling strands V. Tight and virtually scalding roots. Effect supposed to be sleek, gleaming waterfall, but colour more like carrot than conker and texture more haystack than billiard ball.

Climb into slinky lurex tube. Pull on slinky 10 dernier hint-of-coalmine tights, slip on casual black 'slip on' shoes. Slip over. Bang funny bone. It is really really painful to bang yr funny bone. Shoes def a size too big. Pad shoes with old Kleenex. Pad bra ditto. Dab *Hint of Bluebell* eau de cologne on delicate wrists, flamingo-like neck Etck. Approach mirror with feeling of poise and diffidence. Say 'thrush'.

This is wot I hoped I'd see: tall, slender, glamorous, flame haired temptress.

This is wot I saw: my usual old self with the following additions – orange stripes on mug and wig, large pink blobs on neck and wrists (am allergic to *Bluebell*, then), funny bumpy bust.

Mused on wasted three hrs of young Life. All Basil's fault. Kissing shld be banned.

Oh well, V. Glad I said 'thrush' as might not have noticed spinach stuck to front tooth otherwise. Bit of a Worry though, as haven't had spinach for about five years. Have decided to wear wig as normal, i.e: on top of hed and hanging down at sides . . .

Undeterred. Went to meet Baz. He was waiting under the clock, just as he said. He is always on time. It is V. Lovable.

Why beat about the bush? I thought. I remembered to say 'thrush' as I approached.

He looked a little startled. 'What?'

'Basil,' I murmured, 'it's Leap Year. Today is February the 28th and old tradition has it that it is the day when girls can propose to their beloveds. I know girls are very forward these days, but I am not That Kind Of Girl. I don't expect you to say yes, or no, just now, but I want you to think about it.'

Basil looked baffled. 'Think about what?'

'Um. What I just said.'

'Leap year? But that's only when there are twenty-nine days in February . . .'

Oops. Still, nothing ventured, nothing gained. And I have already Said It.

No more beating about bush. Gulp. 'Basil, listen.'

'Yes?'

'Will you marry me?' Ha Ha   Heh Heh Ha

'Hah a ha ha ha ha ha ha ha ha ha ha ha ha ha ha ha ha ha ha ha ha ha ha hee ha ha hahah ha ha ha ha ha hee hee! Hha ha ha ha ha ha ha ha ha haaaaaa HEH!' (I may have left out the odd 'ha ha ha' or 'Heh.')

I stood blinking like vole hypnotized in headlights and then my legs started running of their own accord. Since I didn't have time to change direction quickly enough, I cannoned into Basil, then spun round and fled.

Heh Ho Ho Ha Ha

Mon March 1
St David's Day
MATHS WORKSHOP

Must concentrate on work, being better person, getting GCSEs Etck, Etck.

Tue March 2
Purim. Feast of Lots
(LOTS OF WHAT?)

Must concentrate on work, being better person, getting GCSEs, finding out what Feast of Lots is Etck, Etck.

Invitation arrives:

> *Gareth & Caroline Appleby*
> *invite*
> *Scarlett*
> *To a Party for their beloved daughter Hazel*
> *SATURDAY MARCH 6th*
> *At home*
> *Eight till late*
> *Dress casual*

Dress casual. Thank God for that, perhaps they are listening to Hazel at last. Still, 'beloved daughter'. Bit gringeworthy. Does Hazel want a party? I doubt it . . .

To say I feel like going anywhere, ever again, wld be to lie.

Oh well, will go to provide moral support and hope not to get ham in CD player like last time.

Now must concentrate on work, being better person, getting GCSEs Etck, Etck. Goodbye, fun.

Wed March 3
BABYSIT

Must concentrate on work, being better person, getting GCSEs Etck, Etck. Am busy concentrating on werk, being better person Etck when doorbell rings. Benjy tucked up in bed sleeping like Benjy.

Well . . . I shout through letterbox that I can't let anyone in cos of the Rotweiller.

But it's Basil.

Heart thudding like a thousand buffaloes Etck.

Open door on chain.

'Letty, let me in. I'm sorry. I must explain.' He holds out a vast gold box covered in tinsel pom poms and displaying the legend: *Gumboil Confectionery*.

'Oh. Chocs. Thanks. I'll give them to my gran.' I snatch them, pushing door against his foot.

'They're not chocolates. Look.'

I look. It is a box of fudge. My heart melts. This is the first person in my life who has given me fudge without me asking. (Well, OK, apart from Hazel. Once). My defences are down. I let him in.

'Letty, I've got terrible hassles at the moment. That . . . mission I mentioned to you . . . things are coming to a head. I think I'm going to have to be away for quite a while, the others feel that the time is right. But I'll be in touch. When we're ready to move, I'll send for you.'

A tingle shoots up and down bony spine of El Chubb. My huffiness about our last meeting and his reaction to my proposal is beginning to melt. His old magick is stronger than ever. Yes! I know I will be with Basil as his hour comes, as he becomes Hero of Werld, releasing us from slavery and tyranny of arms business and corrupt governments!

'I feel . . . You're . . . the only one who understands me . . . the only . . . person I can trust. I wasn't laughing about us being together for ever, please believe me, it was just to cover my fears for your safety if you come with me into the dangerous world which destiny has made for me. But we will meet soon, and all will be revealed.'

Even bigger tingle shoots up spine at thorts of what this statement cld mean.

'Can I leave some stuff with you?' Basil continues quickly. 'While I'm away? Just a few bits and pieces, precious things?'

'Well, OK. But how do I know you mean it – about what happened?'

'You have to believe me. It's been hard for me to

198

understand that someone as – young, as byootiful – as you could possibly show an interest in an old warhorse like ME.'

'You're not THAT old!' I cry. 'And I'm not that young.' (pushing out chest in sultry manner)

'I'm 22, Letty.'

This did take me back a bit. I'd put him at 19, tops. Somehow he seemed to have insinuated himself into the house and onto the sofa, where I seemed to have joined him.

'Letty, darling, will you wait for me?'

'Basi . . . mmnnffff.'

'Letto, what that man doing in your jumper?'

Getting Benjy back to bed took another half hour, by which time Basil was pacing about.

'It's just as well your adorable brother came down Letty. He's so gorgeous – I might have gone too far. And you are too young . . .' he murmured, tempestuously.

It was my turn to feel anxious about the poss turning of my father's key in the lock. 'Yeah. You'd better go.'

'Will you wait for me?'

'Spppflmmmmmnhglurg.'

'I'll drop round next week with my stuff. I'm going the week after that. But we'll go out, before I go?'

'Yes. Yes. Come to Hazel's party on Saturday.'

'Er . . . I'll be away. I told you.'

'Oh. Yeah. What about the 13th? We're all going to a dance, at the scouts' hall.' (The scouts' hall. Great.)

'Of course. Yes. Let's meet there and then, you know, go on somewhere?'

YES YES YESSS. *Go on somewhere* . . . He loves me. He loves Benjy. He loves fudge. He'll even come to the scouts' hut for a teenage dance! *Go on somewhere* . . . OK, suppose he's even away for a year. What's a little year? I'll be sixteen when he comes back. It'll be legal. Phwoor. I'll wait. Hell can freeze over.

Thur March 4

Oh wot a byootiful week. Tra la la. Tra la lee.

Am interviewing Syd Snoggs today. Will take Aggy along as bodyguard. After all, if round Stanley and Brian can make passes at El Chubb (not heretofore noted for her magnetism in area of boyz) then Syd Snoggs is V. Likely to try and 'give me one' as he so charmingly puts it to every gurl who passes . . . Have arranged to meet him in cafe.

9 pm. Syd Snoggs was in Cholesterol Charlie's cafe with eight mates. At the next table were: his horrible sister Sandra, his horrible brother Dion AND Ruth'n'Van'n'Elsie. Wished I had bought a dozen or so mates myself, but realized I haven't really got a dozen or so mates. Am not a gang person, I tell *moi*self to cheer self up. Anyway, any vain thorts I had of being magnetick with a tape recorder in my hand are kicked

200

well out of touch by old Syd and co.

'Trouble wiv you lot is you think you can just sit back and see the working clarses die for you,' says Syd.

'An' then you can write poems about how terrible it is and CRY.'

'Yeah. It's always the poor bastards who can't afford to get out of the way that cop it. All the poor sods all over the world in uniform who make the world a safe place for the likes of you to curl up by yer log fires havin a snog on the shag pile.'

'Wiv us acourse, it's a shag on the log pile, but it's more fun.'

'Well, my GRANDAD was blown apart in 1945 and never even got to see my mum.'

'And my dad's in the back of a truck on his way into the Current Situation RIGHT NOW. An I hope he kills enough bleedin' khazis to come home safe.'

'Er, yes . . . but . . .'

'But WHAT?' they all say, fixing me with gimlet eyes like a bunch of ancient mariners.

Yulp. What can I say? Decided Syd undoubtedly has a point. If people in yr own family have to go to war, it entitles you to say your piece about it more than most. Funny to feel more at home with Syd and co than with Brian. Would, in fact, rather be called a poncey middle-class wuss than a bleeding heart liberal. Although it might be qu nice not to be called either.

But that's what's so wonderful about Basil. I don't know what it is he's doing, but he's trying to make a difference.

Have one more go: 'Look, I take your point, I really do.' (Realize am sounding totally snotty and try to smile, by whispering 'thrush' under my breath, which obv gives me V. Weird expression cos they all strain forward quite sympathetickally as I struggle on.) 'But could you just answer this question one by one?'

Grudging nods.

And then I asked: 'Do you think it's a good idea to drop bombs on babies?'

Syd Snoggs: 'Well, not as such . . .'

Dion: ''Sokay if they're khazis. Stops 'em growing up to drop bombs on you, dunnit?

Winston: 'Don't pay no attention to him. He's only taking the michael. Course not. Only a loonie'd do that.'

Arthur: 'Never. I'd never kill little babies.'

Ruth'n'Van'n'Elsie: 'Wotchyou think we are? Psychos?'

Sandra: 'You're disgusting. Who'd do a thing like that?'

I don't answer. I'm trying to work something out. All I can hear in my hed is the voice of Josef, but I know I can't say anything. I just don't know how to put it.

Ruth'n'Van'n'Elsie: 'Go on, why'd you ask?'

'Well, I'm not trying to be clever. Really, I'm not. I just think what you've said proves that most young people don't think it's a good idea to drop bombs on babies.'

'Oooh. Ain't you clever? Ain't she clever? Ooooh.'

I soldier on: 'And, most young people say they wouldn't do it.'

'So what's your point?'

'Um. But that's what a whole lot of young Brits like us did in Dresden in the Second World War, and a lot of young Americans did in Vietnam, and a lot of young Russians did in Chechnya. I mean, they wouldn't have wanted to, either . . .'

Silence.

'Yeah. Well, it's orders, innit?'

'But they've got a point, haven't they?' muses Aggs, on the way home.

'I know, I know,' I mope.

In fact, I am secretly pleased. Surely these guys will add the antidote to bleeding hearts Etck. Also, they will show up Brian. Heh! Heh! My film will be the best! I will make loads of dosh!

Midnight: Sat up late editing tapes of Syd and co.

We are going to show the rough cuts tomorrow prior to a public showing next week. I KNOW mine will be the best. Art is a wonderful thing.

Fri March 5
FILM COURSE

Made a little speech about my film:

'I have developed a, um, theory that individuals are

203

usually peaceable, thoughtful and gentle,' sez I. 'The trouble starts when we form into mobs, groups, gangs, parties and armies. Under orders from somebody else – who might be wrong, or mad – we can do things we'd never take responsibility for on our own. So, er, this is why they always use several blokes in a firing squad and give one of them – but no-one knows who – a dud bullet. So no-one has to take the blame, see? So if we could all act as individuals and listen to our consciences there would be NO MORE WARS.'

Sit down, rather shakily, realizing that this argument is shot with holes, so to speak. After all, NOT all individuals are OK. What about how you deal with mad axemen? Some of them don't seem to respond to a cosy little fireside chat and a pat on the back. Also, how wld we have won World War 2 Etck? However, speech has such gude effect that I sublimate my doubts and sink into rapturous state of self congratulation. Ooh, clever old *moi*.

'That's great, Letty?' sez Dot (I put a question mark in to show she is Australian cos all their sentences sound like questions).

'Brilliant,' sez Oliver.

'Ooh Letty, you're a gem,' sez Saul Spangle. And gives me a big hug. I glow.

'Letteeee 'as summed up so much of what weee aaallll waaant to say about ze state of ze nation and huuuuman natuuuuure,' sez Alfonsa.

YES!

We watch all the films. There is no doubt. Mine is the best. And there is no doubt either about its star, the very twinkling Basil. Wish I had got him to take off his shades, but the old dimples twinkle, the old cleft twinkles. He twinkles all right. And sounds so bloody intelligent. Got to hand it to him. He is bloody intelligent.

'Wheeeerrre you get heeeeem?' purrs Alfonsa. 'Eeef only all young men had hees breadth, heeees underrrstanding, hees wwee . . .' (I had a horrible feeling she was going to say 'willy' here, but thank goodness, not) '. . . eesdom.'

But she keeps me back after the class.

'Letteee, yorr feelm weel win ze prize, you know zat. But to make eet really beeg, we could get eet into the National Feelm Theatre Young Directors show, and for that eet weel haff to be a leetle shorter. I know eet ees harrd, but you must cut a leetle somsink.'

Of course, I had already cut it down to the bare bones, using snippets of all the best interviews and running the whole of Josef and Basil. Surely she didn't want me to lose Basil? I couldn't bear that.

She meant I should cut Josef. She said he was very moving, in his way, but he had no 'screen presence'. His stutter and his poor command of English made it difficult to understand what he was saying. There were too many pauses.

'But he's the only really real person in it,' I stammered.

'Lettee, I sink I know best. If you cut heem now you

can do heem again in another feelm, only better.'

I could see her point.

I said I'd think about it.

Sat March 6

Today's the day. The Applebys' party for Hazel. Go round early. Hazel and Aggs are already togging themselves up.

'At least Brian won't be mooning about after me, now I've told him it's all got to be platonic,' I said. 'Which will leave the way clear for Gorgeous Baz, Heh Heh Heh.'

Aggy gulped and sniffed.

'What's wrong, Aggs?' I said, all jolly and full of glee.

'You're so insensitive sometimes, Letty,' seethed Hazel 'Can't you EVER see things through anyone else's eyes?'

'*Moi*, insensitive?' I cry.

But instead of joining merrily into the joke, Hazel and Aggs just luked daggers and Hazel put her arm round Aggs and offered her a bit of pink loo roll. Aggs blew her nose.

'Bit early for hay fever,' I said, my jollity evaporating like burst balloon being burst. 'Well, sorreee. But I'm not telepathic. Forgive me for not seeing exactly wot is UP. But you know, if there's something wrong, please feel free to share it with me.'

'You are SO full of yourself! You just don't see what's in front of your nose!' said Hazel, suddenly furious. 'You didn't even realize that Basil didn't even fancy you at first. It was ME who he blew a kiss to at the New Year's Eve party.'

This stopped me in my tracks, I must say. Of course, Hazel had been standing right next to me at the New Year's Eve party. And anyone with half a gnat's brain can see that if curvy golden-wigged sparkling eyed Hazel is standing next to stick insect, wholewheat spaghetti-wigged Chubb, who would be most likely to get a kiss blown at them by Basil.

I winced as I remembered his first phone call (it is etched in my brane): '*Letty, I know you love Adam, but when I saw you at the party I thought, Adam is a fool. How can he pass up on such a gorgeous creature?*' When we had those first phone calls, he must have thought he was talking to someone who was called Letty but luked like Hazel. And I chose to think he thought I was gorgeous . . .

Then I remembered he hadn't recognized me at the airport. He pretended it was his shades. Felt nasty, very nasty, pang as I recalled the luke of disappointment flitting across his manly brow. Sat down, rather fast, on bed.

'Oh,' I said, articulately. ← ARGHHH!

But worse was still to come. Hazel in Basil's flat . . . Had they had a tryst after all? Was Mandy a cover all along? Were they stringing me along all that time? Felt nauseous as hope and trust ebbed along with my Life Bludde.

The silence that followed seemed to last for several hours, although I could tell afterwards it was only seconds. Hazel moved towards me in slow motion, like an action replay, only much much slower. A look of guilt and shame suffused her beautiful mug.

'Oh, but he obviously does fancy you now,' she said. 'Sorry. I was cross.'

'Did you spend time with him in Scotland?' I flash with icy flash.

'Of course not. He came by once to collect his

post. But that was it, he was there five minutes. And . . .' Hazel tails off alarmingly.

'What? What?'

'He . . . um . . .'

'WHAAAAAT?'

'He asked me to deliver a few parcels for him,' Hazel admitted in the end.

'Oh, did he? Where to?' I squeaked.

'Strange places. I was a bit scared going to them, but I thought I should because he'd been so helpful to me. And also, you know, because he obviously had Serious and Important Work. I mean, he is a Man of Mystery, isn't he?'

'He is,' I sighed. 'But what do you mean, "strange places"?'

'Dustbins downtown, holes in walls, wastebins in hamburger joints, ugh.' Hazel wriggled her nose. 'Weird. But he said it was all a secret part of his business and he'd tell me one day.'

'One day!' I squawked at her.

'Well, it's just the kind of thing boyz say,' Hazel said, patting my arm. 'But it's nothing. You know I don't fancy blokes, and so does he.'

I wondered for a moment just how and why the byootiful Hazel had been able to make this so clear to him.

'Well, then why are you telling me this?' I ask, furious. 'Why are you so cross with me?'

'Because it should be obvious to you that Aggs is really upset because she likes Brian.'

Umph.

Have spent my life wishing Brian and Aggs wld like each other to get him off my back but have been so put off him by his views on war that now I couldn't imagine anyone wanting to go out with him.

'Oh. Aggs. Do you? Really?'

Aggy sniffs hard. 'I do, as it happens. And you're so vile about him.'

'Well, um, he was so nerdy. When I interviewed him, I mean.'

'Yes. Well he's very young. You know boys mature slower than girls. He's also very brainy, and very sensitive and I . . . I just won't go to the party if he's not there. What's the point?'

'Oooh, Aggy, you must come. I know, I'll give old Brian a ring.' Felt a complete toe-rag. Of course I must perswade Brian to come. OK, one woman's meat is another's poison and so on, but the happiness of a frend is more important than anything. I think.

I phone Brian.

'Hi. It's me. Letty.'

'I KNOW.'

'Just wondered if you were coming to the party tonight – er, only I-I've got a surprise for you.'

'Ooh. Yes. I was, actually, um, anyway.'

'Er, you um, do understand what I told you, about being platonic, don't you?' I add, as afterthought, not wanting him to get wrong impression Etck.

'Yesssss. See you laterrrrr. Grrrrr.'

He's so weird.

Went in to break the good news to Aggs.

'Phew. He sounds really pleased I rejected him. He's probably had his eye on you all the time,' I told her. 'But maybe you should think again about those sateen culottes.'

We tried a few outfits on Aggy but decided the sateen culottes were better than squeezing into slinky lycra style tube and bulging out either end. Tried to restore her confidence with a bit of, you know, two vast brains together, think what brilliant kids you and Brian will have Etck. Hazel, meanwhile, who hates parties, was dillying about which of her slinky negligees to waft downstairs in and tempt hopeless swains with. In the end, she slipped out of the third slinky wafty number in which she looked a million dollars into dungarees in which she also looked a million dollars.

'It's not fair, Haze. You'd look good in a bin bag with a loo seat round your neck.'

Hazel mussed up her hair. (Question: can you improve a mane that lukes like a silken waterfall? Answer: yes, by mussing it up so it lukes like a tousled waterfall.) 'Who's it for, anyway?' she grumped.

Aggy decided not to wear her specs, so we had to help her downstairs.

Dressed to thrill…

The party:

I told Hazel about my great plan to get Brian and Aggy together.

Then I saw him, luking over with strange simmering luke.

He approached.

'What's the surprise, then?' he said, running his eyes up and down me in an odd way. I hoped he hadn't been taking anything. But my mind was elsewhere (on Basil). I unselfconsciously clasped his hand.

'Brian, I always knew you were big enough for this,' I said, gratefully.

He gulped.

'And you'd be man enough to handle it if I told you how I really felt,' I continued, 'so that's why in a minute I'm going to show you something that will make you really happy,' I promised.

He just stood there with his mouth flapping about like a goldfish.

'It was right in front of you all the time, but you never saw it,' I insisted, knowing my grate plan was going to werk and I cld make two people happy at once.

Brian made an odd gargling sound. 'Er, wot?' he croaked.

'Outside,' I whispered, 'not here.'

'Good,' Brian says. 'There's a lot of people in here with dirty minds.'

'Meet me outside by the oak tree in five minutes.'

And then I ran over to Aggy. 'I've set it all up,' I hissed. 'It's going to WORK!' I shoved Aggs outside and helped her arrange herself in a langorous pose under the oak tree. The first fine drops of rain were gently falling. All the better, I thought, for a clinch to avoid the storm.

Then I dashed back to the house and cannoned into Brian, on his way to the oak tree.

'Letty, Letty,' he lunged wildly, grabbed me and started slobbering on my neck. There was a huge roll of thunder and a flash of forked lightning. It was like being attacked by a werewolf.

'BRIAN! What are you doing?! Have you gone mad?'

'I don't understand. You said . . . you wanted our relationship to be plutonic. You know. Hot, steaming. Volcanic.'

Oh, no.

'Not PLUTONIC. P-L-A, PLAtonic.'

Brian stumbled off, his hed in his hands, bumping into, and ignoring, the half-drowned Aggy on the way.

Arg. Wot utter, utter, failure. Rain now bucketing down. I ran to the tree, but Aggy had vanished. Oh no. She will be distraught. What a total plukerama.

Sun March 7
COOKING, GRANNY CHUBB

Interesting Fact: Telephone Invented on March 7! Well, patented akshully. (NB A patent is a thing you take out when you have invented something to stop anyone else copying it, har har, tell that to bt). It was invented, fascinatingly enuf, by a bloke called Alexander Bell. I spose if he'd been called Alexander Wind that the voices of our belurveds wld be preceded by gales of farting noises.

Rang Aggy first thing. Her father sez she's in bed with flu. Suppose Aggy gets pneumonia and dies and it's all my fault? Even if she recovers, which is possible owing to antibiotics, Aggy is bound never to want to speak to me again. She has no self confidence as it is, and to be completely ignored by Brian, when she was hoping for an evening of rapture Etck. I know what she will be thinking – that she is worthless pustule on humanity's bottom.

Ask G. Chubb wot is good for flu and she sez, let's cook nourishing vegetable soup. Can I bring any nourishing vegetables my mother has around the house? Find two potatoes, can of baked beans, half a pack of frozen peas and saddish looking onion. Granny Chubb thrilled. She has most of her monthly carrot and a small bit of cauliflower, so we can make a good soup.

Take a bowl round to Aggy.

Tiptoe up, expecting werst.

Aggy is lying prone in bed, her face to the wall. The only sound she makes is a light snuffling. The room is dim. I turn on the light, and realize it is on already. Ten-watt bulb. Aggy makes no move. Her heart is broken. And it's all my fault.

'Aggs, it's me,' I gulp.

'Letty!' she sez, sitting up bright as button. 'Thag you, thag you, thag you a thousand tibes.'

'S'only soup,' I blush.

'No thag you! Thag you for chadgig by LIFE.' (She is thanking me for changing her life? It is like Ophelia. She has been driven mad, by love, or by flu. But she is quite obviously barking.)

I take a step backwards. 'Er, no, it's just soup, really.'

'Dot the soup! Briad! It worked!' She has gone all soupy. She is soupier than the soup.

Anyway, to cut a short story long, Brian had hurtled past Aggy and she, quick as a wink, had hurtled after him. All she could see, wot with the rain and no specs, was a speeding blur, but she recognized his nerdy Where's-Wally-style scarf. Just as she closed on him, he tripped on said soggy scarf and she fell on top of him. And one thing led to another.

'I love hib,' snuffled Aggy dreamily. 'Ad he loves be.'

Oh Gawd. Another possible astrophysicist brought

216

down by the hungry claws of the biological clock. Or something.

Mon March 8

Josef has not been in school for a week, and he was not in today. No-one has asked where he is. He didn't make any mates and no-one seems to have noticed. I finally asked Ms Farthing, who said he'd been moved. Apparently they're trying to split the refugees between more skules to even out the GCSE league tables or something, and Sluggs already has more than its share.

'But he's had such a terrible life,' I say.

'I know, Letty,' she says, kindly, 'I know.'

She says she will find out where he is and I can write to him if I want. Maybe Ms Farthing isn't all bad after all.

This evening was one of those ones where Mother got it into her hed to read Benjy an improving buke. Tonight, it was *Alice's Adventures in Wonderland*.

Mother: Chapter one: Down the Rabbit Hole . . . Benjy, look at the lovely rabbit.

Benjy: Why's he got a clock onner string?

Mother: That's an old-fashioned pocket watch darling, called a fob.

217

Benjy: Fob?

Mother: Yes. Fob.

Benjy: Fob. Fob, fob, fobbetty fob. Har har di har.

Mother: (thinks: he has such a wonderful imagination, he loves to discover the beauty of langwidge. I think he will be a great writer or, perhaps, poet) Yes. Fob. It's a lovely word isn't it?

Benjy: Fob. Fob, fob, fobbetty fob. Har har di har. Fobby slobby blobby FOB.

Mother: (patience very slightly strained) Look, Benjy, Alice is sitting by her sister on the bank, and . . .

Benjy: What bank?

Mother: The river bank, I suppose . . .

Benjy: What bank do you keep a couple of squid in? A river bank. Har di har. FOB. How long is a giant squid's testercles?

Mother: TENTACLES. I don't know. Look it up in your encyclopaedia. Now listen, Benjy, this is a very exciting story. Alice goes down a rabbit hole! And has lots of tremendously exciting adventures. With caterpillars! And walruses! And . . .

Benjy: Snot very excitin. I've seen the film. 'Sgot a lot of cards runnin about.

Mother: That's just the *Disney* version. That's nothing like the book. This is proper literature, Benjy. (Trying V. Hard to keep calm) Alice is on the bank. And in her own mind, she considers . . .

Benjy: In her own mind? How cld she consider in someone else's mind?

Mother: Don't try to be clever with me Benjy!

But Benjy is now engaged in furious fight with his duvet, which has turned into a giant squid.

Benjy: Help, help, call Captain Nemo.

So ends another educational episode in 21st centurye Britain.

As I lie awake, I think I have made a really hard decision. I will phone Alfonsa and let her choose the cuts for my film. Will say, cut Josef or cut Basil. S'up to you. I can't make the decision. Her experience must surely be greater than mine.

Tue March 9

V. Scary thing happened today. Mr Proton put V. Evil-luking flask of bubbling liquid on his desk and told us on no account to touch it as it wld burn our insides out. He turned away and, in the two seconds his back was turned, Jack Spriggs put another, identical-luking flask next to it! Then, just as Proton turned, he leapt towards the flasks, said that life had dealt him one too many blows Etck and he had to End It All and took a vast swig from the wrong flask and fell writhing in agony. Spiggy fainted and the rest of us were hysterical, I can tell you. Proton clasped Jack to his manly chest and forced some antidote down his gob while Aggy rushed to call an ambulance. The manly chest of Proton was more than Spriggy could stand though and he sprang back to life. What? Eh? Turned out he is not only an ace joker but an awesome sleight-of-hand king, too. He had switched the flasks so ALL of us thort he was drinking the wrong one.

The ambulance team came in useful for Spiggy and Proton, whose nerves were in shreds.

We spent the rest of the Science lesson werking in silence on inventions. Feel me and Aggs cld be the perfect team for science. Her brains, and my imagination.

Here are just a few of our inventions, which we are planning to submit to the **Teenage Think Tank**, if only the govt wld get off its bum and set one up:

The Aggy-Chubb fax mobile. This disassembles person or object into component parts, and faxes it straight to its destination. Haven't quite werked out formula for reassembling molecules at exit, but Aggy is werking on it. Our first try was with a rubber (not Jack Spriggs's pet one, of course), which exploded so we have decided not to try it on anything living until govt funding available. Syd Snoggs exploded a beetle, but Aggs and me have now banned him from experiments.

The hedometer. Lukes just like normal thermometer but zooms up to dangerous fever level in two secs. Limited use of two goes per student each term, as danger of discovery under the eagle eye of Mrs Hornet otherwise. Priscilla Crump used it four times last term, but she was poorly, so I took pity. Turned out to be having twins, in fact.

The two-minute tampon. This is so absorbent that it just takes out a whole month's bludde at a time, so you only have to wear it for two mins and that's your period over. Still in development stage, but Aggy sez we will need vast iron supplies to go with it, to avoid fainting from anaemia. So might be better to market it with couple of girders attached.

Stretcho-mug. Elastic face you can just put over your usual one, for parties Etck. Choose any luke. Or you can even luke like yr self, if you want, but without plukes, blemishes Etck.

Magnetick butes. This was Jack Spriggs's idea. You have to have cunningly placed magnet on football, too, for them to work. In theory, the ball just goes straight to your bute, wherever you are on the pitch. The left bute has an attracting magnet and the right bute has a repelling magnet, so the right bute scores. Spriggy and Spiggy appeared to both be wearing attracting magnets as they werked on this together, giggling, before she fainted and he was dragged off to dungeon.

Bull-e-meter. Not to do with mad cows, unless you include Ruth'n'Van'n'Elsie. This lukes like normal skule pencil (ie: small blunt wooden stick that gets smaller, but not sharper, when introduced to blade of any kind) which emits a piercing shriek if there's a bully in vicinity. Still unreliable at present as it went off when only little Armand from Yr 7 was in the rume. He had to be sent home for a week with shock.

Wed March 10
BABYSIT

Jack Spriggs has been excluded.

I get up a petition for him. Am qu pleased with it akshully.

We, the undersigned, wish to protest at the exclusion of Jack Spriggs from Sluggs. Jack was only having a bit of a laugh and did no real damage. He did not mean to make Sarah Spiggot faint and has already told her he is very sorry. He has also sent a letter of Apology to Mr Proton.

Me, Spiggy and Aggs went round the whole skule getting people to sign it. Even Ruth'n'Van'n'Elsie signed up *and* Syd Snoggs. Jack is the kind of boy everyone likes, even teachers. Maybe if the petition doesn't werk, we shld let on what goes on in Proton's krap science lessons. But we are not completely thick. It never does to grass on a teacher, no-one believes you.

Thur March 11

Interesting Fact: First English Daily Newspaper The Daily Courant published on March 11 in 1702. Wonder what raisin they had to call it a currant, arf arf. This led, inexorably (NB New Werd, meaning unavoidably) to ye gutter press of ye 21st century. But I expect they thort it was gude thing at the time and more reliable than gossip over garden fence Etck. Wrongggggg.

My Mother is having another go at wading through *Alice* with Benjy. This time she got as far as page three, where Alice is falling V. Slowly down the rabbit hole and sees a jar marked orange marmalade. Alice is V. Disappointed to see it is empty at which point Benjy lost interest completely and started another duvet fight. Maybe *Alice* shld be updated to say peanut butter, or Strawberry Angel Delight. It's hard for Benjy to identify.

But he still came into my rume at 3 am wailing, 'Was chased by giant Wabbid!'

'Er, wot?'

'Giant wabbid! Hobble big floppy ears!'

'Oh. Rabbit.'

Calmed him down with midnight pillow fight.

You'd think my mother wld know better than to read something about rabbit holes to a kid with floor phobia.

Fri March 12
FILM COURSE

I am a hero.

Basil is a hero. My film is unberleevably good. And Basil's interview sends shivers down everyone's spine. Alfonsa has definitely made the right decision. The film has everything. It is moving, it is funny, and it moves along really fast now. It's very sad to lose Josef, but I will do him again, when I have time and money.

'Thees ees sso gooood Letteee, that the feelm buffins weeel lerve it. Maybeeee it weeeel go to the beeeeeg feeeeelm festivals!'

I cannot wait to tell Basil. And soon, in just one little day, he will BE THERE!

Sat March 13

OOOH, ooh ohh. Today's the day. Dance at the trendy scouts' hall . . . The going on somewhere of Letty and Basil . . .

Only spend two hours getting ready for dance. Don't want to outshine Aggy, har har. But anyway, Baz has seen *moi* several times now and seems not to be too put off.

Junior's band were playing. The Mandibles are, in fakt, a grate band. You will hear them soon on *Top of the Pops*, mark my werds. Sort of cross between early Chumba Wumba, recent Will Smith, extra-depressed version of Oasis and the late grate Sid Vicious singing *My Way* while eating packet of tortilla chips.

Junior plays bass guitar and sings. He is about eight foot tall and ten foot wide with massive dreadlocks and a voice like diesel engine on cold day. But gentle as a lamb, according to Aggs.

Aggy and Brian smooched Worryingly in the

corner, while Hazel, Spiggy and me did a little dance routine I'd worked out in front of the mirror. It's the one where you put your right elbow in, your right elbow out, blah. Only I've added a bit more:

(to the tune of hokey cokey)
You put your right elbow in
You put your right elbow out
You clap your hands together
And you shake your wig about.
You waggle both your eyebrows
Then you rub them on your knees
You scratch yourself all over
As if you have the fleas
— and that's what it's all ABOUT.

Ruth, Van'n'Elsie were doing a rival dance on the other side of the hall, just like *West Side Story* (not the dance, the situation). They kept pushing their bazooms out and hiking up their skirts, it was V. Naff. And gradually, everybody except two or three blokes who like to be thort of as Ladz (obviously readers of *Wet Shellsuits*) came over to our side of the hall. That's because our dance is one everyone can do. You don't need a single BIT of skill. It's a great dance cos it's so nerdy it zooms out of nerdsphere, bypasses cardigansville and zaps straight into kool sphere without missing a beat. To prove it, even the break dancers were joining in.

But while I was waggling an eyebrow here and

there, I was keeping my peepers skinned for Basil. Eventually, even this dance can make you hot, so I slipped out and saw Basil himself, leaning V. Coolly against a wall with slight smile on face, as if above all our childish poncings about.

I screeched to a halt. He saw me, came over, whisked me into his tongue and stayed there for five hours. So that's a knee trembler. (No, I think a knee trembler is not just a kiss. Must check.)

He said he had a little bit of business to wind up but why didn't I go back to Junior's for a night cap? He'd see me there at 10.30, but remember, he had to catch plane at 4 am.

Oh, so this was 'going on somewhere'.

A nightcap. A night cap? A cap? For the night? Oh, no. Not a contraceptive cap? Glanced at my watch in a blurry daze. Not five hrs then. Five seconds.

But, help. Going to Junior's is also going to Basil's.

Torn between longing and terror.

Not sure if akshully ready for complete bedrume scene, *moi* thinks.

At 10.30 we all piled out of the fab scouts' hall and up the road to Junior's (and Basil's, swoon).

Brian and Aggy disappeared Worryingly into Junior's bedroom. Was just wondering whether to follow to make sure Brian was not in officer-material mode and ordering Aggy to undress, when Aggy hurtled out, weeping.

'You've got to come home with me. You've got to!'

'What's up?' Even Brian couldn't have done anything that bad, that quick, surely?

We leave together and then she unclasps her hand and reveals . . . her charm bracelet!

'No! Where was it?'

I pieced the rest together from Aggy's sobbing account. Brian had pulled her onto the bed, knocking over Junior's bedside table as he did so. The drawer fell open and out fell – Aggy's bracelet.

Arghhhhh!

'Not Junior! A thief?'

'Yes, Junior!' (sob sob) 'And I've known him all my life!' Aggy collapsed on the pavement.

'Aggy! It's not that bad.' (It was, ackshully.)

'No, it's my foot.' She had got her foot stuck in a drain. There are a load of kids round here who prise off drain covers. Why?

I heave her up.

'What are we going to d-d-d-d-d—?' (sob sob sob, more bog roll – lucky I have some stuffed in my bra for uplift) 'do?'

Grasping at straws, I say, 'Maybe he got it off a fence.'

Blank look from Aggs. At least there are some things that pass V. Brainy people by.

'A fence is someone who buys and sells from robbers. So he might have bought it off a robber and sold it to Junior, who bought it in all innocence.'

'No. No chance. Junior knew all about my bracelet. All my mates did. He'd have recognized it.'

So. What are we going to do? Shop Junior? Get Ruth'n'Van'n'Elsie to come round and duff Junior up with menaces? Confront Junior on our own?

'Well, we obviously have to tell the police.'

'NO NO NO. He's an old FRIEND!' (sob sob)

'Well what then?'

'We'll have to think.' When Aggy's majestic brain starts working it always amazes me. Her whole body changes. She grows a couple of inches and loses about two stone. It's like watching Clark Kent turning into Superman. I wish I cld X-ray her head and watch all the little cogs and wheels spinning and all the circuitry flashing. 'Leave it with me,' she says. 'I'll call you tomorrow.' And she is off, into the night.

Of course, I hare back to find Basil.

But stop at door realizing I can't face Junior.

I ring from phone box.

No-one ever answers the phone when they've got about twenty people in their house. Oh, oh, oh. Basil is off on his Grate Mission to Save The World tomorrow and now he will think I Don't Care. Scrawled a note in eyeliner and shoved it through the letterbox. Something like:

Love you. Emergency cropped up. See you the minute you get back - Letty.

Sun March 14
Mother's Day, UK

Arg. Did I write 'Love you'? I am mad.

Sloped down to breakfast with hangover. Too much Fanta.

Heard sad little voice humming glumly from kitchen, thus:

'Happy Mother's day to me
Happy Mother's day to me
Happy Mother's day dear me-eeeee
Happy Mother's day to me.'

Streaked upstairs quick as a weasel and rummaged round rume. Find *Bluebell* scent. YES. Only a teeny bit used, owing to allergy. Top up with tap water. Sneak into parents' rume where father snoring. Too much Fanta. Go to mother's present drawer. Grab tissue. Wrap scent. Tear off one of dad's envelopes in which he gets his werk returned with letters that say: 'Thank you for letting us read your novel/play/article on plumbing. We are sorry to say that it is not right for our list/theatre/journal. Good luck in your future attempts and don't give up the day job.'

Use cardboard to make V. Wacky abstract design out of lipstick Etck. Stick on bit of wool and corner

230

of bedspread. Lukes just like one of Benjy's collages. Decide, in fit of nobility, to let Benjy sign it too. Horrible Father shld have reminded us about Mother's Day, so it's not Benjy's fault. Congratulate self on selfless behaviour. Waltz downstairs with Benjy.

'Happy Mother's day!'

Benjy is also clutching Bogey and Fartles which he thrusts at Mum.

'Oh. Benjy. How Lovely! Are you giving me Bogey and Fartles?' Benjy looks doubtful. 'But of course I wouldn't take your bedbums.'

You bet she wouldn't. Trying to get Benjy to sleep without Elly, Bogey and Fartles wld be like trying to get Granny Gosling into a fast-food joint without a blindfold and a peg on her nose.

'And what a LOVELY card. You are a clever boy.'

After about five hours she notices my present. So much for selfless behaviour.

Aggs rings and we meet in the park. She is desolate. She has always thought of Junior as a big brother (you'd think five siblings would be enuf, but who am I to say?) Betrayal is a terrible thing. But, because of her sentimental, or just plain mental, attachment to the past, she cannot bear to tell the police yet. She wants to give Junior a chance.

I'm not too keen: 'Anyone who can do that to an old friend is a complete creep,' I say, eloquently.

'No, Letty. He must have been desperate. There

must be a good reason.' A glance at my dropped jaw. 'I know it's hard to think what, but we've got to try. So I'm going to send him this. What do you think?' She pulls a note from her pocket:

Dear Junior,
I found my charm bracelet in your room. Unless you return all the other things you stole from my family (or their cash equivalent) by 6 pm on Wednesday, I will inform the police.
Agatha.

Well, what could I say? She'd made up her mind. It was her bracelet. And her things. And Junior was her friend.

Aggy folded this note carefully (I like the 'cash equivalent', I would never have thought of that) and we went round to Junior's. He always plays with the Mandibles down at the Duck & Unicorn on Mondays, so we knew he wouldn't be home. But I'm Unsure this is the right course of action . . . If only I could tell Basil. He'd know what to do.

Mon March 15
MATHS WORKSHOP

Horrible thing happened today. Aggy and me skipped maths workshop only to see that Junior was lurking outside the school. Went straight back and did maths workshop, sweating. Should we tell the teacher? Decided not, as Junior would surely have given up by now, thinking he'd missed us. But he was STILL THERE when we came out. Subduing surging Panick attack, Aggy and I sneaked out the back way, over the caretaker's roof and through the junkyard. I walked Aggy home. Then she walked me home. Then I walked her home again. No sign of anyone, so I left her, telling her to tell her dad about it and on no account to open the door.

I really want to talk to someone about this. But who?

Arghhhhh!

Tue March 16

Sleepless night. V. Releeeeved to see Aggs at skule. She said Junior had called her last night but she'd refused to speak to him. He called twice more and eventually she went to the phone and shouted down it: 'If you call me again, I'll tell my dad everything.'

'You mean you haven't told him?' I was horrified.

I really wanted someone to know about this apart from me and Aggs.

'Junior's dad was my dad's best friend. It would break his heart.'

But at 3.45 Junior was outside the school, waiting for us, AGAIN.

We got out over the caretaker's hut again, although this time he heard us and came lurching out swearing. I wonder if head teachers know the sort of langwidge caretakers use when kids are doing perfectly normal stuff like skiving? Never mind the kind of langwidge used on occasions like when they find you jumping over their roof. Have never run so fast before. Wonder if ticker about to give up ghost. Can you get heart attack at fifteen?

ARgHHH!

I am not enjoying any of this, it is all too Scary. I need to tell Basil, he wld be able to get Junior to leave us alone. I persuade Aggs to spend the night at my place. I'm afraid Junior will stalk her. I say we have to tell the police. Aggy begs for one more night. Her own experiences with the police have not always been V. Good as her two brothers have been picked up loads of times for doing nothing.

'It's because they're black,' I said, grimly.

'Oh,' said Aggy. 'They never told me they were

black. You'd think they would have, me being their sister and all.'

Aggy can be really sarky. I have often tried to wake her up to the inequities of cruel racist werld, but she has always found physics more interesting.

Wed March 17
St Patrick's Day
BABYSIT

St Patrick's Day. Wish I was Irish, or Scottish, or Welsh, or Abyssinian or something. Whoever celebrates anything English? Must find out about St George.

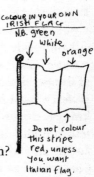

COLOUR IN YOUR OWN IRISH FLAG.
N.B. green
white
orange
Do not colour this stripe red, unless you want Italian flag.

Aggy is staying with me again tonite. I need her to, as am babysitting and V. Scared of being on my own.

'We HAVE to call the cops this time, Ags,' I say.

'Yes, we'll call them at 6 pm but not before. It takes time to get cash equivalents, and I'm going to keep MY word. I said 6 pm and I'm sticking to it.'

We bunk off skule an hour early to avoid bumping into Junior again and go round back alleys through the dreaded Gradgrind estate. Usual wailing of sirens, breaking of glass Etck and it's only 3 pm. See Benjy's little mates Duane and Bugsy playing in a skip with an axe.

'Not at school, Bugsy?' I grimace.

'Nah. Bin excluded fer nickin biscuits.'

'That doesn't seem a good enough reason to get excluded,' I say to him encouragingly.

'Nah, well the 'edteacher was eating 'em at the time,' Bugsy announced unconcernedly. 'D'yer want some?' He pulls a mashed digestive with little bits of fluff clinging to it from his sleeve, where there are clearly several more biccies lurking.

I am touched by the offer, but politely decline.

Surely skules aren't excluding six-year-olds? Wot is the werld coming to?

Aggy and I hang out in the park for a bit on the swings, discussing betrayal of old frendz. 'This is where Junior used to swing me,' she weeps. 'He used to put me and Mandarin and Quail on one end of the see-saw and he would go on the other and he was still heavier,' she wails . . . 'That very same see-saw! Still there! After all these years!'

'And never knowing it was hosting the bum of a BUM,' I say fiercely.

'But he was so kind,' weeps Aggy.

I guess if your mum runs off with a postman then one more betrayal is the old straw that breaks the old hump. I hate seeing Aggy so down. I will personally kill Junior, it's the only option. I will kill him and sprinkle him on the window box. Aggy need never know. Aggy's dad need never know. Junior will be one of the great 'disappeared'.

5.55 pm. We go to the phone box. Aggy is trembling like a leaf.

6.01. Aggy rings her dad, to find out if the money's there.
   She puts the receiver down with a heavy hand.
   'No. Nothing.'
   Right. That's it then.

6.05. Ring Aggs's Dad one more time.
   Still nothing.
   We have been more than generous. We have given Junior loads of time to relent and give the stuff back. He is a skunk. But Aggy is still reluctant. Her mind is still overloaded with swathes of happy memories stretching back into babyhood: Junior helping her with skulewerk, buying her birthday presents, more swinging her on swings Etck Etck.
   'I'm surprised those swings are still standing,' I say, feeling the time has come to get a grip.

6.20. I get a grip.
   I am firm, I am bold.

6.22. I ring the cops. This turns out to be a V. Boring and long-winded process where I have to give loads of info about *moi*self, which makes *moi* feel V. Clammy. Then I have to give loads of info on Aggy's robbery, then loads of info on Junior. Then the money runs out. I reverse charges, but the call is not taken.

I look at my watch. It is 6.40 and I said I'd be back at 6.15 to babysit Benjy.

'Oh. Pluke. I'll have to ring them up again from home.'

'No point. You said it all, we've betrayed him now,' hiccups Aggy.

'No. He betrayed you.'

'But it feels so wrong.'

'Never mind, you've got Brian,' I soothe. Oh well.

Decide Aggy must stay at my house again. For my sake as well as hers, do NOT want to be in house alone.

When we get back, my parents are raging, late for some poxy work party. If they only knew my pain and Aggy's pain. They storm off, saying there's only enuf food for me and Benjy and they can't afford to feed the whole class. Bloody rude.

If they only knew.

Plonk Benjy in front of computer. He is now playing GOD II and doing much better than Dad on it, which makes me feel oddly sad.

Tell Aggy she has got to ring and tell her dad everything. The police are bound to call round and he'd better hear it from her, first. She can see the point of this and tells him all. He is heartbroken.

'Surely it can't be true. Old Harvey and Edna would turn in their urns. Little Junior.'

'Not so little now, chum,' Aggy tells him. 'Bolt the door and don't let anyone in! The police will be round soon.' Aggy is in such a state that the minute she's put the phone down she starts Worrying that now her father won't let the police in. 'I must go round and be with him.'

'Aggs. Cool it,' I say, in officer-material tones. 'Your dad is bigger than me and I need you too. Suppose Junior comes round here? Anyway, your brothers are at home and between them they can surely tell the difference between a bunch of cops and a bunch of thugs.'

Aggy lukes at me as if I'd just popped out of an egg.

Decide to make the most of an evening with Aggs. Got Benjy tucked up early. I'm really getting the hang of this babysitting thing now. My Mother gets it all wrong by being either V. Cross or V. Cringing with Benjy which he milks for all it is worth. I have a calm, fair, understanding approach. But just as we settle down to a cosy video and a shared curry-in-a-bag there is an incredible shrill ringing, thumping and walloping. Someone is leaning on the bell and trying to knock the door down. There is a deafening, menacing shout:

'LET me IN! Let me IN!'

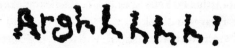

Junior!

We plunge the house into darkness, nearly. You may read about houses being plunged into darkness, but actually it's not that easy. You can't in fact turn all the lights off at once.

We run about like Tom and Jerry pulling plugs. Then we dive under the sofa.

A tempest of blows rains down upon the door. 'LET me IN! Let me IN! I KNOW you're IN THERE!'

'Dial 999. Quick!' squeals Aggy.

I crawl to the phone. Just as I am about to pick it up, it rings.

'Letty, it's me. I'm outside your front door. You've got to let me in. I'm in trouble.' I say nothing and slam the phone down.

'It's not Junior,' I say. 'It's Basil.'

'Could be a trick. You know they sound alike.'

I slither along the floor and try to peek through the curtains. The phone starts ringing again madly (well, brr brr, just as usual, but you know, it feels madder). I crane my flamingo-like neck to no avail, so crawl along hall, through new carpeting of pizza and home improvement leaflets.

Can now hear the voice clearly. It is not being perlite. It is, in fact, in danger of offending the whole neighbourhood. Does sound like Basil, but Aggy's so nervy, I have to check.

'If you're Basil,' I shout through the letterbox, 'then wot kind of bird am I?'

'WHAT? What are you talking about?'

God. Can he really have forgotten comparing me to a flamingo? I suppose he could have. Especially as I suddenly realize he thought I was Hazel when he made that long ago and faraway comparison. Suppress this glumey thort and plunge on: 'What was I wearing at the party?'

'How should I know? Let me in for godssake! This is crazy!'

'What's my brother called?'

'Who cares? I've only met the little bastard once.'

Little bastard?

Doesn't sound like the caring Basil I know and lurve, but still, it is obviously him. Junior has never met Benjy.

Put the chain on door. Open it a crack just to check no-one else is there.

Only a wild-eyed, tousled, flushed, magnificently byootiful Basil. Realize I still have Sluggs uniform on, including naff jumper with egg stains. Oh well. Love conquers all, they say. Open the door properly.

Basil tumbles in. 'Oh, Letty, Letty darling.' Tongue event. This kissing stuff is too much for me. I am a helpless pawn in his lips. He loves me, obviously. Far too much to care about little things like wot I am wearing or my brother's name. Who cares about that stuff anyway. Slip my frantic fingers into his frenzied mane of fudge.

'Oh. Aggy. What a surprise.' He pulls away as Aggy shuffles sheepishly from foot to foot in the hall. 'Look. Letty and Aggy, I need some help. There's some bad vibes from Junior.'

'We know, we know. We've told the police,' I yelp helpfully.

'You've WHAT?' he asks sharply.

'We know about Junior being a thief and that it was him that stole everything from Aggy's,' I say. 'I couldn't wait to tell you.'

'Oh. You . . . you think . . . Junior is a thief,' spluttered Basil, looking relieved.

'Why didn't you tell me?' I ask. 'You know how awful it's been for Aggy!'

'I had no idea,' sighed Basil, a tragic luke suffusing his manly brow. 'But that explains why he's been behaving so oddly. Poor Aggy. A friend's betrayal, when it is of that magnitude, is very very hard to take in.' Basil put a tender arm round Aggy and I saw vibrant flashes of electricity flit briefly between them, resulting in violent pangs of jealousy flitting electrifyingly over *moi*. Basil obviously can't help doing this. He is a kind of sex machine. 'Anyway, my darling,' he turned his hot gaze on *moi*, 'I wish I could stay to help, but I'm catching a plane in three hours. I only came to drop off my stuff. Remember, you said you'd look after some stuff for me darling?'

'Of course. Would you like some curry-in-a-basket?' I alluringly offer.

But Basil is already phoning for a mini cab.

He gives me his holdall. 'Just sentimental, really. Oh, Letty my dearest darling, I'm so sorry about Junior. It's hard to believe. But I'm sure he must have been desperate. I'm sure it'll sort itself out. I'll ring tomorrow.'

Then the cab comes and he is off, in a haze of fudge, Armani and *Eau Barbarique*.

Aggy brings me a cocoa.

We eventually agree that Junior is more likely to be on the run from the cops than coming round threatening us. Anyway, he wouldn't want to face my folks.

'Maybe he *was* desperate,' Aggy sez, hopeful to the last. 'Basil is very caring, isn't he?'

'Yes,' I grimace.

Even so, we wait till my parents weave home (singing loudly, I think I'll have to move house, I can't face the neighbours). We put them to bed before creeping down, double locking everything and piling chairs against the front door.

Thur March 18

Slept for about five minutes. Woke to screams and shouts as father fell over chairs in hall.

'I've broken my effword leg!' he shouts.

That's the second time this month. He soon won't have a leg to stand on. Hah.

'Sorry, we were looking for something,' I mumbled, hoping this wld pass for an explanation. Now 8.35, luckily, so Aggy and me fled to skule before any further argument cld arise.

We race round the corner smack into Junior and three vast blokes. There is a piercing scream. I think it is me.

I pummelled Junior as hard as I could. *Pow. Klang. Bang.* 'Oof! OUCH!' I said, falling back, my knuckles in shreds. I leapt at Junior again, only to find myself grabbed round the waist by one of his huge mates, a bloke the size of Jaws, only not so friendly looking. Jaws thrust a hand in front of my nose. I bit it (his hand, not my nose). But in the same millisecond that I bit the hand, I noticed it was holding an ID card. I've seen them on *The Bill.*

'D.I. Bugcrusher,' he said. 'I should warn you that biting a police officer is a punishable offence.'

I stopped, utterly bewildered.

Obviously, Aggy was right. You can't trust anyone. Even the police were in on this.

But they weren't.

I couldn't believe my ears for a long time, but slowly it all came out.

Junior is not a thief. He had realized who the thief was when he got Aggy's note. He had tried to warn us (ringing Aggy, waiting outside school for us Etck), but eventually he'd called the cops and come round to my place.

Junior tried to tell me the next bit nicely but it was the kind of news you can't break like that.

The thief is Basil . . .

No. No. It can't be, I cry, thrashing about.

But yes, yes, I suddenly know it is.

Aggy was crying with relief and flinging her arms round Junior. I was just crying. They have failed to nick Basil. Partly because WE, stupidly, helped him! Oh. No.

Fri March 19
FILM COURSE

Stay off school. Have endless interviews with the Bill.

Basil, they say, was not a sharp man-of-mystery internet yuppie trying to save werld. He had a part-time job as a cleaner at Gatwick airport. Oh well, he wasn't lying about going off to airports then. That's good.

The stuff about the packages comes out in the end. They ask me about them, but somehow it seems as if they aren't that interested.

Even though I know Robin Hood stole to help the poor and underprivileged, there is now a bigger and bigger part of me that knows Basil is no Robin Hood. But it's worth one more little try . . .

'He was working for a Better Werld,' I sob through tears. 'He was part of a secret movement to

rid the Werld of Pestilence and War. He was trying
to do Gude. I delivered packages (well, one
akshully, behind a dustbin) to his frendz in the
movement, but I never saw them and I don't know
where they are.'

'A parcel like this?' D.I. Bugcrusher asks me,
rather sneerily. He is holding up a package like the
one I dropped for Basil, with his handwriting on it.
It has been opened. Aaargh! My heart sinks at what
might be inside. Drugs, I suppose. Or a gun!

D.I. Bugcrusher pulls the package open wider
and sticks it contemptuously under hooter of *moi*.

It is full of torn-up bits of telephone directories.

Oh. How pathetick.

Basil is pathetick.

I am pathetick.

I luke at the policemen with such a luke of
mystification and surprise that they almost laugh,
and then luke sorry for me instead. Maybe they
have hearts after all.

5.00 pm. Have just realized that Alfonsa will be
showing my film tonite, to the entire werld. And
my star anti-war witness is a liar, a thief and a sad,
lonely fantasist who only wants stupid, gullible
twits like *moi* to think he's a Hero.

And I have helped him. Oh, great.

'And he had such a lovely suit and such nice
manners,' was all my mother could say. She is
shamed, naturally.

Ring the New Directions course to tell Alfonsa to drop my film from the showing.

'What rubeesh arrre yoooo talkeeeng Lettteeee? Yor feelm is a meestresspiece.'

'Yes, but—'

'Of course I weel show eeeet.'

'No, Alfonsa. You can't. It's, it's . . .' I can't bring myself to tell her the truth. My tongue has turned into blu-tak and has stuck to the roof of my mouth. I've worked so hard on my film, it's so good.

'Don't be fooleeesh Letteee. You are jussss nervusssss. Everyone weeeel love eeet. I see you there, darleenk. Byeeee.'

A myriad (**NB new werd**, meaning lots) of emotions pass through my feeble frame. I want my film to be shown so badly. I want everyone to love it. I know they will. I know I will win the prize. I know I'll get on the next course and I'll get into film school and leave behind the glumey vista of GCSEs and a life at FATS checkout.

But I know it is not to be.

I can't have Basil speaking out as the honest voice of Love and Peace in a tortured universe any more. Even if no-one found me out – which is possible – I wld feel everlasting shame.

I ring back but NO-ONE answers.

So I have to go.

Dear, kind, faithful, happy Aggs comes with me.

We get to the course just as Alfonsa announces

the films. If mine is showing first, we've had it.
But luckily it is randy Stanley's.

As his film drones on, I step out of the shadows
and pull Alfonsa behind a door.

'Letteee. You are herrre. Wunnerfool. Ze head of
ze Feeeelm Schooool is here. I have told heeem all
about yoooo. Heee weeel lurve ze feeeelm. Hee
weeel be eating from out of my paw. Heee weel
geeve us loads of money. Yoooo weeel be a starrrr.'

I had to listen to this. Trying to stop Alfonsa
when she is in full flow is like trying to stop a
privatized train with only a couple of red lights.

'Alfonsa, you know Basil?'

'Ooooh Baszeeeeel. Ze gorgeous one wiz ze
caramel hair? Yessss! Heee weeel be big starrr.'

'No, Alfonsa. He is a liar and a thief. And his
hair is beige.' I said it. I said it.

Alfonsa stared at me for a moment. But, like me,
she only saw and heard what she wanted to see and
hear at that moment. And that moment passed in
only a moment. Behind her head, I could see my
film was starting! 'Rubbeeesh Lettee. Eef ee 'as
dumped yooo zen I am trroooly sorry, but eet does
not make what eee says any theee lessss
eeemportant! Ee is ze starr of ze show and ze show
muss go on!'

My film was showing. I was mesmerized. There
was nothing more to say.

The room shimmered with a collage of familiar
scenes and sounds . . . my dad's voice, reading the

poem, Brian (I could feel Aggy gasp, then wince), Daniel, so arrogant, the nerds at the tube, bits of the army recruitment film, Syd Snoggs, shots of young men dying . . . then Basil. So fluent, so articulate, so expressive, so convincing, so breathtakingly handsome . . .

I was deafened by the applause.

Through the buzzing in my brain I was dimly aware of the film school head exclaiming in rapture and asking to meet me. I could feel various hands patting me on the back. But all I felt *inside* was dust and ashes. If this was triumph, then what was failure? How could I have done it? How could I have betrayed Josef by cutting him out? His, and his alone, was the Real Face of War.

I couldn't face Oliver, or Saul, or any of them. Aggy propelled me in front of her ('She's not well, gotta take her home') out of the room, into the street, into the tube and we rumbled home. From time to time she hummed a happy hum. She is so happy about Junior. Then she remembered and gave me sad anxious looks.

What is worse? The betrayal of an old frend? Or of a new love?

Or of a boy you never really listened to and never really knew, but who knew more than you could ever know?

Oh Josef. I'm sorry.

Benjy has to sleep with me as he has lost his beloved Fartles.

Mother has turned house upside down.

Try to get five mins with her to pour heart out, but all she can do is Worry about Benjy and Fartles.

What is worse? The betrayal of an old frend? Or of a new love? Of a refugee? Or the loss of Fartles?

Sat March 20

2.30 am. Cannot sleep. Suddenly remember Basil's holdall. It is stuffed behind the sofa. Oh, oh oh. Maybe it wasn't all fantasy. Perhaps this is the real thing. This is the drugs, or the guns??! Perhaps he is a master-criminal after all, and this was going to be the payoff, once he had fooled everyone he was just a saddo with the dummy packages and stuff. And he'll be back for it. Aaargh! Now this IS Panick.

Supposing it's full of drugs? I'll be an Accessory after the Fact. I'll be jailed in jail for the rest of my young life, only allowed out when I'm an old woman of forty, to roam the streets gazing bleary-eyed at the young folk, skipping merrily about, children I never had, Worrying about their stupid spotz.

Do not dare to go down and look in holdall.

2.35. Must go down. Can't go down. Think am getting flu.

2.38. Make self a cup of hot lemon *Hooterhug*. Fill hot water-bottle. Realize have filled bottle with *Hooterhug*. Is this how madness starts? Am drawn as if by magnet to sofa. Cannot face it. Wake up Rover. Ask her advice. This is what she sez: *Meeeeeeee sngggmmm*. She sleepwalks onto my hed and settles.

Right. Obviously there is a Meaning here. The werld of Catz is saying: Go to sleep or you will wake Rover. Think about the bag tomorrow. So I will.

2.45. Bag bag baggety bag. Holdall.

2.52. Triple Pluke! Suppose it's full of explosives! He works in an airport! He could be an undercover terrorist. Suppose the whole house goes up while I yam asleep? I must face it and risk banana to save loved ones.

2.58. Tiptoe down, Rover still on hed (I don't know how she does this, but she does). Take bag. Drag it through kitchen and out into back yard. If it explodes when I open it then at least only I will die. Remember Rover. Remove her from nut (hard, as she clings on with claws like vampire bat even in deepest slumber) and carry her, still hibernating, to sofa. Say tearful farewell.

'At least you cared, dear Rover. You stood by *moi*.' Bend to give her a little kiss.

Then I stagger out, sneezing, into dark, freezing yard.

Close eyes.

Unzip bag.　　**Arghhhhh!**

Hold breath.

Well, you know I wasn't blown up, of course, else I wouldn't be writing this. But I did not know. I was V. Pleased akshully, which, even in my fevered state, I noted as a Good Sign. I have not lost the will to live. What I saw, not good however. Once again, Basil proved he is not a man to take for granted:

Bag of white powder, obviously drugz.

And two or three long, hard, scary metal objects, wrapped in cloth.

Far too scared to look closer. If there are gunz and drugz . . . might there be bombs too? Well, even *moi* thort this unlikely. Even a luny doesn't need to blow up the Chubb hovel. But I took no chances. I poured four buckets of water into the bag.

3.10. Shove bag into dustbin.

As I do, I notice prone squirrel. It doesn't luke at all well. I make it little snack. I remember all the hedgehogs I must have killed when I was younger by giving them bread and milk (milk V. Bad for digestive systems of hedgehogs).

I put little bowl of nosh in front of squirrel and then realize it might not be its front, so put another little bowl behind it. Then think, maybe that's not its front either, maybe it is facing other way and when it wakes up, too sick to move, it will not see food and DIE.

Put two more saucers of nosh out, so now squirrel is surrounded on all four sides.

Creep, weepy and shaking, upstairs. Thinking, at least I have done something to help poor little creatures of werld, just like Basil said he would. Hypocrite!

6.30. Wake, trembling. I must have flu. My forehead is like a furnace. Can only think of squirrel. If squirrel alive, everything will be all right. Maybe it was all a bad dream anyway.

Creep downstairs.

Please, let there be no squirrel, no holdall, no Basil.

I see a little prone form surrounded by saucers.

The dawn light reveals it is not a squirrel.

It is Fartles.

Oh.

What will I do?

Have flu.

Sun March 21

No cooking. Temp 103.
  Am dying.

Mon March 22

Temp 103.
  Benjy brings me a card: I will draw it for you here.

*Translation: "Get well now" (not 'soon', you note –
Benjy remains bossy, even when V. Simpathetick)*

"I miss you. Tons of love, Benjy." Sob. Sniff. Etck

He also gives me a little lumpy parcel wrapped in newspaper and bound up with a whole roll of sellotape.

When I open it, it is Fartles.

'Why you cryin Letto?'

'Just got sellotape in my wig. Not to Worry,' I croak.

Tue March 23

Temp 103.

Wed March 24

Interesting Fact: (No, not interested in anything, anything at all. Still, Scotland and England were united today in 1603. Not for long. Hah!)

Temp 101.
   Take little light broth.
   Hazel and Aggs come round. Do not speak. They stand luking Worried.

Thur March 25

8 am. Temp 99. Meant to get it back up so as not to face werld but mother had not refilled my hot water-bottle for a day and a half, so nothing to heat it with.
   BUT.
   Oh no.
   Returning to ghastly reality reminds me of The Holdall! I have been harbouring drugz and guns!
   I have!
   I must tell someone.

I burst into tears.

V. Worried, but driven by mad ravings of El Chubb, Adored Father calls D.I. Bugcrusher to say I have further information. Tries frantically to call his lawyer whilst waiting for cops to turn up, but same is in bed with a hangover apparently. They were at university together, and seem to have started life with the same bad habits – it's just that the lawyer went into a business where you can stay in bed and get paid more.

D.I. Bugcrusher comes round with D.I. Barnacle. She looks embarrassed and offers me a cough drop once she hears me trying to splutter my announcement. Weird.

'No, no, I must confess,' I cry.

'Not without a lawyer,' snaps my dad. 'He'll be up and about in a brace of shakes.'

Three hours later, the lawyer arrives, carrying vast, Worrying pile of law books. His name is Geoff Rabbitt.

For a while, it's pretty difficult to get down to the Awful Business, because G. Rabbitt and Adored Father spend about nine hours joking about 'Hair of the Dog', what happened to old Biggles 'Zappa'

Bloxworth and his collection of 8000 Mothers of Invention records, and whether Geoff's acting his own 19th divorce case or paying somebody else to do it. The police start to get a bit restless after a while, though I think it's the persistent sobbing and sniffing of *moi* that finally brought Solicitous Geoff and Adored Father back to the point.

G. Rabbitt leafs Worryingly through his law bukes and coughs loudly whenever I try to speak. But all his cautions cannot stop *moi*.

I tell them all.

The cops looked miffed, to put it mildly.

'You put it in the bin? And forgot about it? When do the bin men come?'

The joy of a reprieve is singing in my hed. They cannot charge me if there is no bag. Can they?

We all hurtle out in the back yard.

But the bin men come on Friday mornings.

So the bag is there. Sodden, covered in slugs, but there.

The whole lot of us go down to the police station. The neighbours have a field day, flapping their curtains like flags. Adored Mother is distraught, but wears luke of one who is trying to keep her hed while all about her are losing theirs.

They all go off to put on forensic gloves or something and rummage around in the bag.

After what seems like hours in which I suffer full blown Panick-attack, they return. Bugcrusher is smiling. Is he a sadist?

Barnacle puts her hand on mine and gazes meaningfully into my eyes (I think this is wot is meant by a soft cop). 'Letty, did you hide any more of Basil's things, honestly?'

'No, no, no,' I sob.

'Good,' she smiles and squeezes my hand. 'You can go now. We will not be pressing charges.' No? Why not? 'The bag Barrington left with you contained nothing suspicious.'

'But what about the drugs? And the guns?'

'Soap powder, a week's washing, and golf clubs.'

The golf clubs were stolen, though.

11 pm. Have tried really hard to understand all this, but it makes my brane hurt. Could my imagination, impending flu and the darkness all have conspired to make me think golf clubs were rifles? Surely not?

But then I did think Fartles was a dying squirrel . . .

Basil, most pathetick saddo of all time, still had to keep up this Man-of-Mystery routine. Even with his old washing and a few nicked golf clubs that Solicitous Geoff said wld have had him laughed off any respectable golf course in the country. Maybe he even convinced himself that what was in the bag was the essential survival kit of a Man with a World-Saving Mission.

Now, of course, I will prob never know.

And I don't want to know, either.

Fri March 26

Interesting Fact: Sad day for music Lovers. Ludwig van Beethoven died, 1827. (NB extra Interesting Fact: Beethoven was deaf, so stop whingeing about yer musick practice and be thankful you can hear. Er, if you can).

Look at first note above with weary cynical eye. Was there a time when the holidays were fun? Long ago? Before I became a Teenage Worrier?

Manage to drag self to skule for last day of term . . . Have to get bukes Etck as am going to spend entire Easter hols under yoke of homewerk.

Aggs and Brian canoodling(!) at lunchtime. All she thinks about is boyz. Wish had left more of his interview in film. That wld have really put her off. But, of course, she thinks she can change him, just like Mum does with Dad . . .

Went for lonely walk round playground, when was

260

hit on hed by stone. Was wondering whether shld boil Ruth, Van'n'Elsie in boiling oil or just tar and feather them when familiar voice said: 'Read it.'

It was Jack Spriggs.

'Sorry,' he grinned his charming lopsided grin, 'didn't mean to hit you.'

I looked at feet and saw pebble was wrapped in paper. Which said: *How about a bit of the other? Or, if you prefer, a little outing to a film?*

I laughed.

'Spiggy's over there,' I said. 'D'you want me to deliver it?'

'You've hurt my feelers,' said Jack. 'It's for you.'

'For me?'

He blushed.

And so did I.

Sat March 27

am. Mother slamming cupboards again. She is in a bad mude cos Dad has gone off for a 'Writing Weekend'.

'I wouldn't mind, if he did some writing when he got back.'

'He does his best, Mum,' I sadly say.

'His best is not good enough.'

pm. I told Jack I needed a little time to think about it. Hurt his feelers. Nice.

Sun March 28
Palm Sunday
COOKING, GRANNY CHUBB

Spend all day with G. Chubb and Benjy recapturing lost Yoof by painting faces on eggs. We will roll them down little hills at Easter and then jump up and down on them.

Have decided, must learn something from Life and gain shred of self-respect Etck. Cannot go out with Jack Spriggs, charming lopsided grin or not. Cos charming lopsided grin of Sarah Spiggot got there first and I do not want to steal Her Man.

Well, I do akshully.

But I won't.

Mon March 29

Interesting Fact: Scott of the Antarctic, who we met earlier in this riveting survey of Interesting Facts, wrote his last diary entry on March 29, 1912. And who can blame him?

Only Father returns from 'Writing Weekend' and retires to bed with flu.

'TSD,' mutters Mother.

Luckily Granny Chubb is visiting.

'What's that dear?'

'Taken Suddenly Drunk,' sniffs Only Mother,

slamming cupboards. Granny Chubb slides smoothly into her role as a full-time nursemaid. I get home from skule to find her sitting beside Father and reading to him! Hah! Father will spend the next few days sweating, shivering, sleeping or on the loo. Even less chance for *moi* to examine plukes, dye wig, weigh self Etck.

No wonder he is poorly. He has just returned from a nightmare of interllekshual hi-achievement. Frank LeSpeaking was speaking. So was Pullova Offhed and Rusty Salmon. Enuf to make even a grate brain sore, never mind the fluffy little one lurking inside dear Only Father's nut.

'Didn't they give you any proper food? You need brain food for a thing like that,' asks Granny Chubb, pale with anger, but spoonfeeding him with boiled egg and soldiers as she speaks. (The writers only eat humus and whisky, apparently.)

Mother eventually persuades Dad to go to the Doctor.

The doctor, interestingly, says Dad has flu.

'Disappointing,' sez my Mum. 'I hoped it wld be something that you could only catch within fifty feet of Pullova Offhed and that you would never be allowed to go within her orbit again.'

Whoops.

Aggs phones, in tears.

She's split up with Brian.

'No!' (yippeee) 'Why?'

'Priscilla.'

'Priscilla!' What can Priscilla Crump, teenage mother of twins, have to do with it?

'Remember what she called her twins?'

'Oh. Something weird. Sounded like a soft drink and a medicine.'

'Exactly. Rabina and Barin.'

'So?'

'Think, Letty.'

I thought. Suddenly it hit me. Uh. Oh. Anagrams of Brian. More or less.

'NO!' I squeaked.

'Yes!'

Tragick walk in park with Aggs. Pooooor Aggs. I tell her she is better off without him. Imagine the Mad-scientist-father-of-two headlines that will follow them everywhere.

Anyway, he is a creep.

'Letty, I love him.'

Knew this was bad move. It doesn't matter how much of a creep yr frend is in love with, you have to never akshully say it.

I tell her about Jack Spriggs. And that I don't think I can go out with him cos of Spiggy.

'Oh, Spiggy's not like that about Jack at all,' sez Aggy. 'They're just good mates.'

'Really?'

'Really.'

Oooh.

Tue March 30

Sleepless night. Half thinking about Jack Spriggs, half about Basil. Terrified at own stupidity, falling for petty crook. Apparently he didn't even own that dump in Edinburgh, was just minding it for some other saddo. And I agreed to carry parcels for him! Could have been much worse than drugs. Could have been bombs! Wake in cold sweat.

And what greets me at breakfast? A letter from Basil:

Dearest Letty,

You will by now perhaps not be thinking very highly of me. I want you to know I have done nothing you need be ashamed of. I cannot explain everything now, but I will, one day, and you will see I have been the victim of a cruel conspiracy.

But first, I want you to imagine something just to help you understand the tortuous decisions that a man like me, who has the cares of the whole world on his shoulders, might sometimes be forced to confront.

Imagine you are an attractive young girl from a Third World peasant community. If you are lucky you will get sold into prostitution. As a result, you will support your whole family until you suffer a lingering banana (he didn't write that, I put it in), *in your twenties, of AIDS. A couple of hundred dollars will buy you land that will support a family of eight in a small holding. You are offered ten thousand dollars to carry heroin in your stomach to Australia.*

What would you do? Where does probity lie in such a situation?

And suppose you just might have something to do with British Intelligence, and have to do things that looked bad, but were for a greater cause than your own little life?

What would you do? Sometimes, to be a true Warrior for Peace, it is necessary to do things you would otherwise believe to be wrong. The end justifies the means. I know you will understand.

And at least you Letty, and you alone, can believe in me. Baz

I am shaken.

Is Basil a romantik Robin Hood after all? Trying to help the poor of the world by wotever means possible? Is he an MI6 agent? Would that be good? Or bad? Will he be caught? If he is, will I care?

Midnight. New Werd: probity (pronounced like 'probe', not problem) means honesty. Hah. Have thought hard about all the thingz Basil has said and written. But I can't make it right again. Realize it is all complete delusion. He doesn't know I've found out that his stupid packages were just old phone directories. He's just a small-time crook with Big Ideaz, trying to prove he is an anti-arms-dealer Zorro figure. But really, he's a tragick control freak who wants to draw innocent Gurlz like *moi* and Hazel into his delusional werld. All right, everything he said about war was true. But only that. He is an airport-cleaner and a petty crook.

If I could write to him I'd say: I don't believe in you, Basil. If you cared about Third World peasants you could join Amnesty or something. Armani suits don't help Third World peasants. Stealing from Aggy's dad doesn't help Third World peasants. Trying to stitch up Junior doesn't help Third World peasants. Wrecking my film-making career doesn't help anyone. You do have to break eggs to make an omelette but the end does *not* always justify the means.

1 am. I'm sure he needs help from someone who can understand what has made him do the thingz he does. It's just that I know now that person isn't me.

2 am. More importantly, I have realized that my own biggest betrayal is of Josef. If I had included him in my film, it would have really meant something. And I was lured by Basil instead. How stupid can you get?

Wed March 31
BABYSIT
AGGY'S BIRTHDAY: GURLZ NITE OUT

Babysitting cancelled as Mum and Dad NOT Speaking since writers' weekend-fiasco. Hooray! (Not that Mum and Dad not speaking, but means I don't have to barter away umpteen evenings of my life to get out of babysitting.)

Spend three hours doing fantastic card for Aggs. Being creative is my only solace just now. Have cut out vast snap of Aggs and slimmed her down a bit by cutting off the edges. She looks a bit wobbly but not as wobbly as usual, arf, arf. Have pasted on pix of all her favourite things and people (Einstein, Pythagoras, Fermat, list of all the chemicals and elements known to humanity, quarks Etck). Realize it is a bit short on gurlz, so add Simone de Beauvoir, Toni Morrison, Aretha Franklin and Pocahontas as last-minute Aggy-style heroines. Had to squash them in the corners a bit but quite a good overall effect.

Aggy V. Weepy when Hazel and me go to get her. One ray of sunshine is, at least her mum remembered to send her a card. You'd think, shacking up with the postman wld make her a good correspondent, but no.

'And this,' said Aggy, sobbing louder.

Her mum had also sent a little silver mushroom.

Had grate nite out with Aggs and Hazel.

Haze was amazed by father-of-two Brian news.

She is luking much better.

'You're looking a lot better, Haze,' I say, as we stuff another doughnut into the weeping Aggy.

'Mandy,' she whispers.

'She's back?'

'Next week.'

'Whoopee! But wot about the older woman?'

'Flash in the pan. Pie in the sky,' grins Hazel.

Aggy cheers up at the bowling alley. She is excellent at bowling, snooker, anything involving calculation of angles.

'I am imagining every pin is Brian,' she sez, scoring her eighth strike of the evening.

I definitely prefer the funny, brainy Aggy to the soupy-in-lurve version.

They perswade me to ring Jack Spriggs.

Well, maybe I will.

Tomorrow, I will.

Thur April 1
First day of Passover

Ring Jack Spriggs.

'Hi.'

'Hi, it's me. Letty.'

'I know.'

'I've been thinking about what you said.'

'Yes?'

'And I thought I'd like to come out with you, um, on Saturday. If you're still interested, that is.'

'Look, Letty. I'm sorry. But I thought you didn't want to. And I'm, er, seeing someone else.'

'Oh. Sorry.'

'Me too.'

'Um, bye then.'

'Cheerio.' (pause) 'Don't you want to know who?'

'Um. No. Yes.' (Spiggy, of course)

'Your mate Aggy. No offence.'

'Oh. None taken.'

'Bye then.'

'Bye.'

I sat down. That's that then. I can't take any more. Another blown opportunity to add to my wasted life. Another betrayal, more deadly than the others. As multiple glume descended, wrapping me in its foggy wings, the phone rang again.

Wearily, I picked it up.

'Hi. Letty. It's Jack.'

'I know.'

'April Fool. See you on Saturday.'

Well, well. Well.

RESOLUTIONS UPDATE

Nope. Whoever keeps Resolutions longer than MARCH!!!?

But I do have an **arsenal** of **new werds**:

The pen is mightier than the sword Etck. Arg. I have been far from *advertent*, when it comes to assessing character. I certainly do not have the *elan* for it on account of being so unberleeevably *naive*. The *decimation* of my dreamz of film-making has left me almost *destitute* of ideaz, and robbed me of a career that seemed otherwise to be heading for the *stratosphere*. I may *feign* happiness and play at being an *aesthete*, but I *imbibe* now from the well of glume. At least I won't get *swacked* drinking only my own tears, but it means I can kiss goodbye to *affluence*. WHY oh WHY did I listen to the *oleaginous* Basil, *inexorably* luring me on with his *myriad* ravings? Certainly, one thing he was lacking in dollops was *probity*.

(If you can do a better few sentences using all the above, send it to me c/o the publisher).

271

Think I need to make NEW resolutions akshully if I go on with this diary:

* Pass GCSEs.
* Do Not succumb to Pretty Faces.
* Try to limit thinking about Boyz to once daily.
* Etck Etck Etck.

Also, write to Josef, try to interview him properly and TELL THE WERLD HIS STORY.

And one thing I resolve never to lose is HOPE. I can see all kinds of silver linings already. Though, of course, as all Teenage Worriers know, Every Silver Lining has a Cloud.